陳久娟◆編著

這就是你要的

單字書

+ + + The Very + + +
# Vocabulary
# Book

MP3

世界上最齊全的單字書當然是字典囉！
可是，學單字總不能抱著字典從A背到Z吧，
第二頁背完了，大概第一頁也忘得差不多了。
本書依各種情境將單字分門別類，順著目錄翻下去，
就可以很快找到您要用的單字，還可以順便將相關的單字瀏覽一遍。

學單字不必太刻意．

這就是你要的單字書／陳久娟編著. -- 初版.
-- 新北市 ： 雅典文化，民 100.07
面； 公分. -- （全民學英文系列：26）
ISBN⊙978-986-6282-39-3 (50K 平裝附光碟片)
1.英語　　2.詞彙
805.12　　　　　　　　　　　　　　100008584

全民學英文系列：26

這就是你要的單字書

編　　著	陳久娟
出 版 者	雅典文化事業有限公司
登 記 證	局版北市業字第五七○號
編 輯 部	22103 新北市汐止區大同路三段 194 號 9 樓之 1
	TEL ／(02)86473663
	FAX ／(02)86473660
劃撥帳號	18965580 雅典文化事業有限公司
法律顧問	中天國際法律事務所 涂成樞律師、周金成律師
總 經 銷	永續圖書有限公司
	22103 新北市汐止區大同路三段 194 號 9 樓之 1
	E-mail: yungjiuh@ms45.hinet.net
	網站：www.foreverbooks.com.tw
	郵撥：18669219
	TEL ／(02)86473663
	FAX ／(02)86473660
出 版 日	2011 年 07 月

Printed Taiwan, 2011 All Rights Reserved

序

　　世界上最齊全的單字書當然是字典囉！只是，學單字總不能抱著一本字典從A背到Z吧，第二頁背完了，第一頁也忘得差不多了。有個字不會拼，手邊就算有本英文字典，又能從何查起？

　　這是一本單字書，你也可以把它當成一本字典，只不過這本字典不是從A排到Z，而是依事件、空間、物品……等各種情境做分類。想知道轎車、跑車、掀背式車款、兩門式轎車、四門式轎車怎麼說，翻看「交通工具篇」就可以得到所有的答案。家庭急救箱打開來，每一樣物品該怎麼說，查一下「日用品篇之生活用具—急救箱」便能一目了然。談到女性話題時瞧一瞧「美容保養篇」，讓你的談話更有深度。跟外國網友聊到"今天是下著毛毛雨的天氣"，找一下「報刊新聞篇—氣候報導」就知道毛毛雨原來就叫做drizzle。

　　擁有本書，您就擁有另一個學習單字的option(選擇)囉！

Unit 1 日常生活篇 016

Unit 2 吃喝玩樂篇 ······ 083

Unit 6 校園單字篇 …………………… 181

Unit 7 報刊新聞篇 ⋯⋯⋯⋯ 193

Unit 8 商用單字篇 ⋯⋯⋯⋯ 228

Unit 9 **數字篇** …………………………… 254

Unit 12 常識篇 …………………………… 291

Unit 1 日常生活篇

衛生清潔用品

tissue, tissue paper	面紙，衛生紙
toilet paper	衛生紙
facial tissue	面紙
garbage can, trash can	垃圾桶
soap	肥皂
soap dish, soap container	肥皂盒
shampoo	洗髮精
conditioner	潤絲精
bath foam	沐浴乳
mouth wash	漱口水
towel	毛巾
shower cap	浴帽
toothpaste	牙膏
toothbrush	牙刷
dental floss	牙線
nail clippers	指甲刀
ear pick	耳挖
nail file	指甲銼
cotton swab	棉花棒
Q Tip	棉花棒
	(品牌名延伸)
pumice	浮石，磨腳石
shaver	電動刮鬍刀

razor	一般刮鬍刀
replacement blade	刮鬍刀替換的刀片
blade	刮鬍刀的刀片
nose hair clippers	鼻毛剪

浴室設備

showerhead	蓮蓬頭
faucet, tap	水龍頭
bathtub	浴缸
towel rack	毛巾架
mirror	鏡子
toilet	馬桶
water tank	水箱
shower curtain	浴簾
dryer	吹風機
ventilator	抽風機
fan	抽風機

家電用品

radio	收音機
air freshener	空氣清淨機
VCR; Video Cassette Recorder	
	錄放影機
CD player	CD 播放器
electric radiator	電暖爐
heater	暖爐
TV set	電視機
washing machine	洗衣機
electric fan	電扇

fluorescent lamp	日光燈
vacuum cleaner	吸塵器
cleaner	吸塵器
vacuum	吸塵器
thermos	熱水瓶
water heater	熱水器
air-conditioner	冷氣
central air-conditioner	中央空調
stereo set	音響組合

廚房設備 - 電器

microwave oven	微波爐
electric oven	電烤箱
oven	烤箱
grill	烤架
electric roaster, roaster	烤爐
toaster	烤麵包機
coffee maker	咖啡壺
electric coffee pot	電咖啡壺
electric coffee percolator	過濾式電咖啡壺
dish washer	洗碗機
dish dryer	烘碗機
electric cooker	電子鍋
automatic rice cooker	電鍋
rice cooker	電鍋
electric stove	電爐
stove	火爐

fridge	冰箱
refrigerator	冷藏室
freezer	冷凍室

廚房設備 - 用具

pan	平底鍋
frying pan	煎鍋
cooker	鍋子
wok	中式炒鍋
pressure cooker	壓力鍋
griddle	煎餅的淺鍋
slow cooker	燉鍋
pot	湯鍋
skillet	煮鍋，有長柄的 小燒鍋
spatula	抹刀，刮鏟
turner	鍋鏟
ladle	長柄杓
ice cream scoop	挖冰淇淋器具
wooden spatula	木製飯杓
frying spoon	炒菜勺
draining spoon	漏匙
skimmer	漏勺
filter	濾器
funnel	漏斗
electric mixer	攪拌器
grater	擦碎板，磨碎器
nutcracker	堅果鉗

blender	果汁機
whisk	攪拌器
mixer	果汁機，攪拌器
kettle	水壺
jug	涼水壺
tea pot	茶壺
coffee pot	咖啡壺
pitcher	大水壺
bottle opener	開瓶器
corkscrew	軟木塞拔，開酒器
can opener	開罐器
peeler	削皮刀
paring knife	水果刀
cleaver	菜刀
kitchen knife	菜刀
pizza cutter	披薩刀
chopping board	砧板
cutting board	切菜板
sharpening steel	磨刀鋼條
rolling pin	桿麵棍
measure cup	量杯
measuring spoon	計量匙
kitchen scale	廚房小磅秤
BBQ grill	烤肉鐵網
BBQ tongs	夾烤肉的夾子
BBQ skewer	串烤肉的叉子
bamboo skewer	竹叉

廚房設備 - 其他

sideboard	食具櫃
cupboard	食具櫃
sink	流理台，水槽
dish drain	裝洗過碗盤的托盤
strainer	濾網
plastic bag	塑膠袋
paper bag	紙袋
trash bag	垃圾袋
doggie bag	打包袋
foil	鋁箔
aluminum foil	鋁箔
cling film	食品保鮮膜
wax paper	保鮮膜
plastic wrap	保鮮膜
freezer bag, wrapper	保鮮袋
Ziploc	保鮮袋(品牌名延伸)
potholder	隔熱手套
oven mitt	耐熱手套
towel holder	紙巾架
ice cube tray	製冰盒
coffee filter	濾紙
kitchen towel	廚房紙巾

生活用具 - 餐具

tableware	餐具

utensil	餐具
silverware	餐具
stirrer	飲料攪拌棒
straw	吸管
bowl	碗
chopsticks	筷子
chopsticks rack	筷架
dinner fork	餐叉
salad fork	沙拉叉
salad tongs	沙拉夾
two-pronged fork	大叉子
carving fork	大型餐叉
spoon	湯匙
teaspoon	茶匙
steak knife	牛排刀
knife	刀子
spatula	抹刀
utensil holder	刀具架
napkin	餐巾
paper towel	紙巾
dish	深盤
plate	淺盤
platter	橢圓形大淺盤
saucer	醬碟，小碟子
tray	裝托盤
paper plate	紙盤

生活用具 - 杯子

paper cup	紙杯
coffee cup	咖啡杯
glass	玻璃杯
stainless steel cup	鋼杯
mug	馬克杯
thermos cup	保溫杯
wine glass	酒杯
cup	茶杯
mug	馬克杯
champagne glass	香檳酒杯
red wine glass	紅酒酒杯

生活用具 - 清潔用具

detergent	洗潔精
bloom	掃帚
dustpan	畚箕
mop	拖把
duster	雞毛撢子
flyswatter	蒼蠅拍
pesticide	殺蟲劑
bug spray	殺蟲劑
insect repellent	用於戶外的防蟲劑
dust cloth	抹布
rag	較髒破的抹布
deodorant	芳香劑
desiccant	乾燥劑

mothballs	樟腦丸
glass cleaner	玻璃清潔劑
scouring pad	菜瓜布
bucket	水桶
dipper	水瓢
bleach	漂白劑
dry-clean	乾洗
detergent	洗衣粉
fabric softener	衣物柔軟精
non-chlorine bleach	不含氯的漂白劑
clothespin	衣夾
hanger	衣架

生活用具 - 寢具

pillow	枕頭
sheet	床單
bedspread	床罩
blanket	毛毯
quilt	厚被
mattress	彈簧床
single bed	單人床
double bed	雙人床
bunk bed	上下舖是雙層床， 多層床
night stand	床頭櫃

生活用具 - 衣帽間

clothespin	衣夾

coat rack	衣帽架
hanger	衣架
hat rack	帽架
shoehorn	鞋拔
closet	衣櫥
wardrobe	衣櫥

生活用具 - 急救箱

medicine cabinet	醫藥櫃
first aid kit	急救箱
painkiller	止痛藥
Aspirin	阿斯匹靈，止痛藥
cotton ball	棉花球
surgical tape	透氣膠帶
tourniquet	止血帶
bandage	繃帶
Band-Aid	OK 蹦
thermometer	溫度計
tongs	鑷子
alcohol prep pad	藥用酒精片
75% alcohol	藥用酒精
scissors	剪刀
povidone-iodine prep pad	碘酒藥片
hydrogen peroxide solution	雙氧水
ointment	軟膏
digestive	消化藥
painkiller	止疼藥

cough syrup	止咳糖漿
sleeping potion	安眠藥
sleeping pill	安眠藥
vitamin	維生素，維他命
Centrum	善存片，(綜合維他命品牌名)
ice pack	冰枕

生活用具 – 工具箱

toolbox	工具箱
hammer	榔頭，鐵鎚
nail	鐵釘
screw	螺絲釘
gimlet	螺絲錐
nail puller	拔釘器
screwdriver	螺絲起子
wrench, spanner	扳手，螺旋鉗
tape measure	皮尺
nipper	鑷子
pliers	鉗子
ax	斧頭
shovel	鏟子
chisel	鑿子
tape	膠帶
ladder	梯子
electric drill	電鑽
saw	鋸子
electric saw	電鋸

pit saw	雙人用的大鋸
bucket	水桶
rope	繩索
paint	油漆
paintbrush	油漆刷
brush	刷子
paint roller	油漆滾筒
hoe	鋤頭
trowel	水泥刀
pick	十字鎬
pitch fork	草耙
spade	鏟，鍬
plane	鉋子
saw file	銼刀
reaping-hook	鐮刀
rake	耙子
scythe	大鐮刀
soldering iron	焊接棒

生活用具 – 其他

key	鑰匙
rubber band	橡皮筋
flashlight	手電筒
table lamp	檯燈
light bulb	燈泡
lamp	燈
fluorescent lamp	日光燈
filament	燈絲

fuse	保險絲
globe	地球儀
toothpick	牙籤
dental floss	牙線
tooth brush	牙刷
tooth paste	牙膏
table cloth	桌布
match	火柴
safety pin	安全別針

洗衣服相關單字

coin-operated washer	投幣式洗衣機
dryer	乾衣機
dirty laundry	要洗的衣服
soap	肥皂，洗衣粉
softener	柔軟精
bleach	漂白水
vending machine	(洗衣粉)販賣機
wash	洗衣
rinse	沖滌
spin	脫水
fold	折(衣服)
wrinkle	(衣服)變皺
hang laundry	晾衣服
dry clean	乾洗
laundry	洗衣店
cleaner	洗衣店
collect laundry	收集要洗的衣服

iron	燙(衣服)
iron out the wrinkles	燙平
laundry basket	洗衣籃
do the laundry	洗衣
iron	熨斗
ironing board	燙衣板

調味料

seasoning	調味品
salt	鹽
sugar	糖
brown sugar	紅糖
dark brown sugar	黑糖
rock sugar	冰糖
cubic suger	方糖
icing sugar	糖粉，糖霜
pepper	胡椒粉
spice	香料
ketchup	蕃茄醬
cornstarch	太白粉，玉米粉
corn flower	太白粉，玉米粉
salad oil	沙拉油
soy sauce	醬油
chilly	辣椒
mustard	芥末
vinegar	醋
barbecue sauce	沙茶醬
cinnamon	肉桂

star anise	八角
cheese	起司
jam	果醬
butter	奶油
caviar	魚子醬
cube sugar	方糖
ginger	薑
green onion	蔥
spring onion	蔥
garlic	大蒜
basil	羅勒
coriander	香菜
chili	辣椒
sesame oil	麻油
oyster sauce	蠔油
olive oil	橄欖油
sesame seed	芝麻
red chili powder	辣椒粉
pepper	胡椒
sesame paste	芝麻醬

常見食材

minced steak	絞肉
chop	肉塊
meat	肉類
vegetable	蔬菜
sea food	海鮮

主食類

rice	米飯
noodles	麵條
instant noodles	速食麵
silk noodles	粉絲
rice noodles	米粉
strong flour	高筋麵粉
plain flour	中筋麵粉
self-rising flour, self-raising flour	低筋麵粉
wholemeal flour	小麥麵粉
steamed bun	饅頭
steamed bun with stuffing	包子

蔬菜類

dried black mushroom	冬菇
pickle	酸菜，泡菜
mushroom	蘑菇
onion	洋蔥
potato	馬鈴薯
carrot	紅蘿蔔
radish	白蘿蔔
spinach	菠菜
cabbage	高麗菜
cucumber	大黃瓜
broccoli	綠色花椰菜
cauliflower	白花菜
red pepper	紅椒

green pepper	青椒
yellow pepper	黃椒
eggplant	茄子
celery	芹菜
white cabbage	包心菜
red cabbage	紫色包心菜
Chinese cabbage	大白菜
watercress	西洋菜
lettuce	萵苣
baby corn	玉米尖
sweet corn	玉米
corn	玉米粒
leek	大蔥
turnip	蕪菁
okra, lady's finger	秋葵
tofu	豆腐
bean curd sheet	腐皮
green bean	綠豆
red bean	紅豆
black bean	黑豆
red kidney bean	大紅豆
peas	碗豆
dwarf bean	四季豆
flat bean	長形平豆
eddoes	小芋頭
taro	大芋頭
sweet potato	蕃薯

tiger lily buds	金針
mu-er	木耳

水果類

tomato	蕃茄
lemon	檸檬
peach	桃子
orange	橙
star fruit	楊桃
cherry	櫻桃
golden apple	黃綠蘋果
apple	蘋果
pear	梨子
banana	香蕉
grape	葡萄
honeydew melon	蜜瓜
lichee	荔枝
kiwi	奇異果
pineapple	鳳梨
custard apple	釋迦
grape fruit	葡萄柚
coconut	椰子
fig	無花果
strawberry	草莓
mango	芒果

豬

pork	豬肉

lard	豬油
pork pieces	瘦豬肉塊
pork steak	無骨豬排
pork chops	連骨豬排
casserole pork	帶骨腿肉
pork fillet	小里肌肉
pork rib	肋骨
spare rib of pork	小排骨
pig feet	豬腳
hock	蹄膀
pig liver	豬肝
pig kidney	豬腰，腰子
pig heart	豬心
pig bag	豬肚
pork sausage meat	做香腸的絞肉
smoked bacon	醺肉
bacon	培根
sausage	香腸

牛

beef	牛肉
mimced beef	牛絞肉
shoulder chops	肩肉
chuck steak	頭肩肉，筋油較多
leg beef	牛腱肉
ox tail	牛尾
ox heart	牛心

ox tongue	牛舌
roll	牛腸
cow heel	牛筋
honeycomb tripe	蜂窩牛肚
tripe	牛肚

雞鴨鵝

egg	蛋
chicken	雞肉
fresh grade leg	大雞腿
fresh grade breast	雞胸肉
chicken drumstick	小雞腿
chicken wing	雞翅膀
duck	鴨肉
goose	鵝肉

海鮮

lobster	龍蝦
shrimp	蝦
prawn	蝦
peeled prawn	蝦仁
king prawn	大蝦
shrimp	小蝦米
dried shrimp	蝦米
crab	螃蟹
crab stick	蟹肉條
oyster	牡蠣
mussel	淡菜

winkle	田螺
whelk top	小螺肉
cockle	小貝肉
scallop	干貝，扇貝
cod	鱈魚
haddock	鱈魚
hake	鱈魚類
tuna	鮪魚
trout	鱒魚
carp	鯉魚
plaice	比目魚
herring	鯡
mackerel	鯖
salmon	鮭
eel	鰻
octopus	章魚
dressed squid	花枝
squid	烏賊
cod fillet	鱈魚塊
smoked salmon	燻鮭魚
herring roes	鯡魚子
boiled cod roes	鱈魚子
dried fish	魚乾
sea vegetable, sea weed	海帶

烹調的方式

cookery	烹調法
boil	水煮

fry	煎
shallow fry	煎
deep fry	炒
stir fry	炸
scalded	燙煮的
stewed	燉的
simmer	文火燉，煨
braised with soy sauce	紅燒的
braise	燜
steam	蒸
smoked	燻的
toasted	烤(麵包)
baked	烘的(麵包)
grilled	鐵盤烤的
roasted	烤的(肉類)
broiled	燒烤的
drain	撈乾，曬乾
dried	乾的
iced	冰鎮的

食材的處理

shell	剝，剝皮
peel	削皮
slice	切片
shred	切絲
mashed	搗爛的
ground	磨碎的
beat	打

toss	擲
knead	捏(麵糰)，和(麵糰)
minced	絞成末的
chopped	切碎的
diced	切小方塊
carved	切好的
frozen	冰凍的

煮熟的程度

cooked	煮熟的
all cooked	全熟的
all done	全熟的
well done	熟透的
underdone	半生不熟的
burnt	燒焦了的
raw	生的，未煮的
fresh	新鮮的
ruined	食物壞掉了
riped	(水果)熟了
stale	陳腐的，變壞了的

房屋的種類

apartment	公寓
house	房子
flat	一層公寓
cottage	獨棟的屋子
en-suite	套房，房內有獨立的洗手間和淋浴間

shack	棚屋
bungalow	平房，小屋
lodge	看守人的小屋，守衛室
suite	套房，共用洗手間及浴室
building	房屋建築物

室內設備

front door	前門
back door	後門
door knob	門把
door lock	門鎖
window	窗戶
bay window	八角窗，向外凸出的窗戶
air window	氣窗
French door	落地窗
screen	紗門，紗窗
aluminum door	鋁門窗
sliding glass door	玻璃拉門
valance	短的裝飾用窗簾
drape	落地窗簾
curtain	窗簾
blind	百葉窗簾
Venetian blind	活動百葉窗
drainage	排水系統
drainpipe	排水管
banisters	欄杆
cathedral ceiling	挑高天花板

ceiling	天花板
floor	地板
hardwood floor	硬木地板
marble floor	大理石地板

室內外生活空間

entrance	玄關
bar	吧台
living room	客廳
fireplace	壁爐
chimney	煙囪
funnel	煙囪
Japanese room	和室
garage	車庫
mahjong room	麻將房
kitchen	廚房
bedroom	睡房
main bedroom	主臥房
master room	臥房
guest room	客房
child room	小孩
bathroom	廁所，浴室
shower	淋浴
restroom	廁所的委婉語
balcony	陽台
porch	前廊，門廊
attic	閣樓
penthouse	閣樓

stairs	樓梯
spiral staircase	螺旋梯
basement	地下室
dining room	飯廳
reading room	閱讀區，書房
study room	書房
workshop	工作間
working room	工作間
studio	工作室
3 rooms + 1 living room	三房一廳
laundry	洗衣間
walk-in closet	更衣間
garden	花園
cellar	酒窖
pantry	餐具室
parlor	起居室
storeroom	儲藏室

傢俱

light	燈
lamp	有罩燈
desk lamp	桌燈
clip lamp	夾燈
table lamp	桌燈
ceiling fan	吊燈，吊扇
rug	地毯
tapestry	掛畫，掛氈
tile	磁磚

wallpaper	壁紙
wall-to-wall carpet	全鋪地毯
bookcase	書櫃
bureau	臥房用衣櫃
chest	五斗櫃
drawer	抽屜
night table	床頭櫃
night stand	床頭櫃
bunk bed	上下雙層床
single bed	單人床
double bed	雙人床
twin bed	兩張單人床
queen-size bed	大號的雙人床
king-size bed	特大號的雙人床
recliner	坐臥兩用椅
sofa	沙發
sofa chair	單人沙發
couch	沙發
cushion	椅墊
love seat	雙人沙發
lounge chair	休閒椅
couch	長沙發，貴妃椅，長椅
bar stool	高腳椅
rocking chair	搖椅
armchair	搖椅
high chair	寶寶椅，兒童椅

stool	凳子
steel chair	鐵椅
wood chair	木椅
desk	書桌，辦公桌等
table	桌子
dining table	餐桌
picnic table	野餐桌
coffee table	大茶几，客廳沙發前的矮桌
end table	小茶几
cocktail table	茶几
folding table	摺疊桌
dressing table	梳妝台
vanity	梳妝台
worktable	工作台，縫紉台
door knob	門把
door chain	門鏈
door bell	門鈴
window frame	窗框
rack	架子
ashtray	煙灰缸
hamper	有蓋的籃子，洗衣籃
plywood	合板，三夾板

親屬關係

great-grandparents	曾祖父母
grandparents	祖父母
grandfather	祖父

grandmother	祖母
husband	丈夫
wife	妻子
father	父親
mother	母親
brother	兄弟
sister	姊妹
elder brother	哥哥
younger brother	弟弟
younger sister	妹妹
elder sister	姊姊
cousin	堂表兄弟姊妹
child	小孩子
children	小孩子(複數)
daughter	女兒
son	兒子
granddaughter	孫女
grandson	外孫子
nephew	侄子
niece	侄女
uncle	伯／叔／舅／姑／姨父
aunt	伯／叔／舅／姑／姨母
daughter-in-law	兒媳婦
brother-in-law	姊夫／妹夫
father-in-law	公公
mother-in-law	婆婆
sister-in-law	嫂子／弟妹
son-in-law	女婿

國家像徵

national congress	國會
national emblem	國徽
national flag	國旗
National Anthem	國歌
national flower	國花
tradition	傳統

季節／氣候

spring	春
summer	夏
autumn, fall	秋
winter	冬
tropical zone	熱帶
subtropical zone	亞熱帶
temperate zone	溫帶
frigid zone	寒帶

時間

time	時間
yesterday	昨天
now	現在
today	今天
tonight	今晚
tomorrow	明天
morning	早晨
day	白天
noon	中午

afternoon	下午
evening	傍晚
eve	前夕
night	夜晚
midnight	午夜
future	未來
age	年齡
calendar	日曆
hour	小時
minute	分鐘
second	秒
moment	片刻
date	日期
month	月份
season	季節
year	年
anniversary	週年紀念日

宗教

religion	宗教，信仰
religious	虔誠的，信奉宗教的，宗教上的
Buddhism	佛教
Lamaism	喇嘛教
Taoism	道教
Islam	伊斯蘭教
Christianity	基督教
Catholicism	天主教

Orthodox Eastern Church	東正教
Greek Orthodox Church	希臘正教
Shamanism	薩滿教，黃教
Judaism	猶太教
Confucianism	儒教，孔教

宗教儀式

pray	禱告，祈禱
ceremony	儀式，典禮
donate	捐獻，奉獻
ritual	(宗教的)儀式
religious rite	宗教儀式
baptism	洗禮
receive baptism	受洗
be baptized	受洗
confession	懺悔
religious service	宗教儀式，禮拜
religious ceremony	宗教祭典
worship	祭拜
attend religious service	做禮拜
go to church	做禮拜
attend Mass	做彌撒
Sunday-school,Sabbath-school	
	主日學 (星期日學校)
sermon	講道
chant	聖歌 歌唱，吟誦 (聖歌、經文等)
meditate	沈思，冥想

meditation	沈思，冥想
ghost	鬼，鬼魂，幽靈
spirit	靈，靈魂

宗教處所

seminary	神學院
temple	廟宇 / 寺(佛 / 道教)
lamasery	喇嘛廟
mosque	清真寺 (伊斯蘭教)
monastery	寺院，修道院
Buddhist nunnery	庵 (佛教)
abbey	修道院
convent, nunnery	女修道院
church	教堂(基督教)
cathedral	大教堂(天主教)
altar	祭 / 聖壇，聖餐台
synagogue	猶太教堂

宗教人物

believer, follower	信徒
Buddhist	佛教徒
Living Buddha	活佛
Buddhist monk	和尚
lama	喇嘛
Buddhist nun	尼姑
Taoist priest	道士
Taoist nun	道姑
clergyman	教士，牧師

rabbi	猶太教祭司
Muslim, Moslem	穆斯林
ahung, imam	阿訇(伊斯蘭教宗教領袖或學者的尊稱)
Catholic	天主教徒
Christian	基督教徒
Pope, the Holy Father	教皇(天主教)
cardinal	紅衣主教(天主教)
archbishop	大主教(天主/基督教)
bishop	主教(天主/基督教)
priest	神父/神甫(天主教)
nun	修女(天主教)
pastor, minister	牧師(基督教)
high priest	大祭司
confucianist	信奉儒教的人
worshipper	參拜者，香客

宗教器具

rosary	念珠
prayer beads	佛珠，念珠
the Bible	聖經
Buddhist scriptures	佛經
the Koran	可蘭經 (伊斯蘭教)
flourishing	茂盛的，繁茂的
incense	香
burner	燈，爐□
snuff	燈花，燭花

049

sedan	轎子
paper money	紙錢
lamp stand	燈台
lantern	燈籠
veil	幔子
altar of incense	香壇
incense burner	香爐
candle	蠟燭
altar	香案
altar	祭壇
Holy Place	聖所
Holy of Holies	至聖所
donation box	奉獻箱，功德箱
shrine	神祠，神龕
ephod	以弗得，猶太教
	大祭司所穿的聖衣
urn	骨灰罈
ash	骨灰，香灰
firecrackers	鞭炮，爆竹

寺廟內景

holy	神聖的，聖潔的
sacred	宗教的，莊嚴的，神聖的
splendid	燦爛的
offering	祭品，供品
tablet	匾額
dragon	龍

phoenix	鳳凰
column, pillar	圓柱，樑
carving, relief	雕刻品，浮雕
eaves	屋簷(常用複數型)
decorate	裝飾
decoration	牌匾

(牆壁上作為裝飾或紀念的金屬薄片或瓷片)

ancestor	祖先，祖宗
God	神，神明
goddess	女神

節慶

festival	節慶
holiday	假日
celebration	慶祝

萬聖節

Hallowmas	萬聖節，11月1日
Halloween	萬聖節前夕，西洋的鬼節
Happy Halloween!	萬聖節快樂！
pumpkin	南瓜
jack-o-lantern	南瓜燈
costume	化妝服
costume parade	化妝舞會遊行
ghost	鬼
vampire	吸血鬼
scary	嚇人的
skeleton	骷髏

bat	蝙蝠
owl	貓頭鷹
goblin	小妖精
witch	巫婆
broom	掃帚
trick or treat	不給糖就搗蛋
knock	敲，敲門
princess	公主
pirate	海盜
mask	面具或面罩
haunted house	鬼屋探險

感恩節

Thanksgiving Day	感恩節
	11月最後一個星期四
Pilgrim	清教徒
Indian	印地安人
The Mayflower	五月花號船
turkey	火雞
mashed potato	馬鈴薯泥
corn	玉米
pumpkin pie	南瓜派

聖誕節

Christmas Day	耶誕節12月25日
Merry Christmas X'mas!	
	聖誕節快樂！
Finland	芬蘭(聖誕老公公的故鄉)

Santa Claus	聖誕老人
reindeer	馴鹿
Rudolph	魯道夫
	(聖誕老公公的紅鼻子馴鹿)
sleigh	雪車
elf	小精靈
elves	小精靈(複數)
present gift	禮物
bulb	燈泡
socks, stocking	長統襪
gingerbread man	薑餅人
candy cane	柺杖糖
Christmas tree	耶誕樹
Christmas card	耶誕卡片
Christmas carol	聖歌，讚美詩
Jesus	耶穌
snow	雪

復活節

Easter Day, Easter Holiday	
	復活節(春分月圓後第一個星期日)
Easter egg	復活節彩蛋
Easter bunny	兔子
flower	花朵
tree	樹木
bird	鳥
basket	籃子

| Easter egg hunting | 找蛋遊戲 |

聖派翠克節

St. Patrick's Day	聖派翠克節
	(愛爾蘭)3 月 17 日
green	綠色
shamrock	酢漿草
Ireland	愛爾蘭
Christian	基督教徒
Christianity	基督教

情人節

St. Valentine's Day	情人節2 月 14 日
chocolate	巧克力
flower	花
lover	愛人，情人
confession	告白

春節

Spring Festival, Chinese New Year	
	春節，陰曆一月一日
Chinese new year	春節
lunar new year	春節
The Spring Festival	春節
lunar calendar	農曆
lunar January	正月
paper-cuts	剪紙
couplets	春聯

firecrackers	鞭炮
dumpling	元寶，水餃
rice cake	年糕
rice ball	湯圓
dragon dance	舞龍
fireworks	煙火
firecrackers	爆竹
red packet, red envelop	紅包
gift money	壓歲錢
lion dance	舞獅
dragon dance	舞龍
traditional opera	戲曲
variety show; vaudeville	雜耍，綜藝秀
riddles written on lanterns	燈謎
exhibit of lanterns	燈會
staying-up	守歲
give New Year's greetings	拜年
taboo	禁忌
family reunion dinner	團圓飯
the dinner on New Year's Eve	年夜飯
rice pudding	八寶飯
candy tray	糖果盤
The Lantern Festival	元宵節
lantern	燈籠

中秋節

Moon Festival	中秋節，陰曆 8 月 15 日

moon cake	月餅
pomelo	柚子
barbecue	烤肉
full moon	滿月

教師節

Teacher's Day	教師節 (中國) 9月10日。 台灣 9月28日
Confucius	孔子
respect	尊敬
make a thank you card	做一張感謝卡

命理

fortune telling	算命
fortune teller	算命師
feng shui	風水
Chinese astrology	紫微斗數
palm reading	手相
face reading	面相
superstition	迷信
Tarot cards	塔羅牌
Twelve Years of Animals	十二生肖
twelve zodiac signs	十二星座
gain good luck	增加運勢
tell your future	測知你的未來
accurate	準確

十二生肖

Twelve Years of Animals	十二生肖
What animal sign were you born under?	
	你屬什麼？
rat	鼠
ox	牛
tiger	虎
rabbit	兔
dragon	龍
snake	蛇
horse	馬
sheep, lamb	羊
monkey	猴
rooster, chicken	雞
dog	狗
pig, boar	猪

塔羅牌

Tarot cards	塔羅牌
Wands	權杖
Ace of Wands	權杖一
Two of Wands	權杖二
Cups	聖杯
Swords	寶劍
Pentacles	五角星
The Fool	愚者
The Magician	魔術師

The High Priestess	女祭司
The Empress	女皇
The Emperor	國王
The Hierophant	教皇
The Lovers	情人
The Chariot	戰車
Strength	力量
The Hermit	隱士
The Wheel of Fortune	命運之輪
Justice	正義
The Hanged Man	倒吊人
Death	死亡
Temperance	節制
The Devil	魔鬼
The Tower	塔
The Star	星星
The Moon	月亮
The Sun	太陽
Judgment	審判
The World	世界

占星

What's your sign?	你的星座是什麼？
character	特質
astrology	占星術
horoscope	占星術
zodiac	星座，黃道帶
twelve zodiac signs	十二星座

fire sign	火向星座
wind sign	風向星座
earth sign	土向星座
water sign	水向星座

白羊座

Aries	白羊座
ambitious	有雄心的，野心勃勃的
persist	堅持
pure	純潔
sincere	真誠

金牛座

Taurus	金牛座
clean definition for people or things	
	對人對事都是愛恨分明
enthusiastic	熱心
kind heart	愛心

雙子座

Gemini	雙子座
sociable	善交際
passionate	多情
unstable	不穩定
clever	聰明
promote	推銷
unpredictable	不可預料的

巨蟹座

Cancer	巨蟹座
motherly love	母愛
family	家庭
defensive	自衛性
romantic	浪漫
sensible	感性
sensitive	敏感，敏銳
picky	吹毛求疵，挑剔
fantasize	幻想
guardian	守護

獅子座

Leo	獅子座
show off	愛表現
passionate	熱情
career	事業
charisma	非凡的領導力
leadership	領導才能，統御力
aggressive	積極，侵略的
acting talent	表演天份
creativity	創造力
self-image	自我形象
self-esteem	自尊心

處女座

Virgo	處女座
sensitive	敏感

cautious	小心
perfection	完美
paranoid	偏執狂，神經質
reluctant	不情願
surrender	投降
calculate	計算
criticism	批評
number	數字
analytical	分析的
financial	金融的

天秤座

Libra	天秤座
fairness	公正
equalization	平等化
motto	座右銘
justice	正義
righteous	正直的，公正的
peace	和平
elegance	優雅

天蠍座

Scorpio	天蠍座
conservative	保守
reserved	沈默寡言的，深沉的
mysterious	神秘感
confident	自信
energetic	精力旺盛

sexually active　　性慾強烈

射手座

Sagittarius　　人馬座，射手座
active power　　行動力
agitated　　焦慮

魔羯座

Capricorn　　山羊座，魔羯座
hard work　　工作認真
mild temper　　脾氣溫和
humbleness　　謙遜
respect　　尊重
stable　　沉穩
proclaim　　讚揚，稱頌

水瓶座

Aquarius　　水瓶座
freedom　　自由
smart　　聰明
sophisticated　　老於世故的
strong ego　　主觀意識強

雙魚座

Pisces　　雙魚座
mild temper　　脾氣溫和
easy going　　隨和
generous　　慷慨
kind　　善良

| quick thinker | 反應靈敏的人 |

逛街購物

boutique	精品店
souvenir shop	紀念品專賣店
duty-free shop	免稅商店
duty-free goods	免稅商品
just look around	只是看一看
window shopping	只逛街不購物
great sales	大拍賣
on sale	拍賣
Can I try it?	我可以試穿嗎？
super market	超級市場
fish market	魚市場
flea market	跳蚤市場
aisle	走道
cart	手推車
trolley	手推車
basket	籃子
section	區域
shelf	置物架
checkout counter	結帳櫃台
counter	櫃台
arrival	新款
best seller	暢銷書
out of print	絕版
edition	版本
new edition	新版

| out of stock | 缺貨 |
| in stock | 有貨 |

尺寸的標示

What size do you take?	你的尺碼多大？
What size are you?	你的尺碼多大？
I am a size 8	我穿八號。
Large size (L)	大號，或以 L 表示
Medium size (M)	中號，或以 M 表示
Small size (S)	小號，或以 S 表示
Extra large (XL)	特大號，或以 XL 表示
Extra small (XS)	特小號，或以 XS 表示

折扣標示

one price only	不二價
10%off	打九折
20%off	打八折
30%off	打七折
40%off	打六折
50%off	打五折
60%off	打四折
70%off	打三折
80%off	打兩折
90%off	打一折
free of charge	免費
special offer	特價

15% off on selected items
部分商品打 85 折。

20% off with this coupon
憑此優待券優惠20%。憑此優待券打八折。

sale	大減價
Half price sale	半價拍賣。
Buy two get one free	買二送一。
trade in	折價換新
clearance	出清存貨
discount	打折扣

付帳

pay	付款，支付
I will take it!	這件我要了！
I'm paying in cash.	我要付現金。
credit card	信用卡
Do you accept credit card?	
	你們接受信用卡嗎？
cash	現金
Cash only.	只接受現金。
tip	小費
service fee	服務費
change	零錢，兌換
installment	分期付款
overcharge	索價過高，多收錢
clerk	店員

討價還價

Cheaper?	便宜一點好嗎？
discount	折扣

這就是你要的
單字書

special discount	特別優待
It's not on sale.	它不打折。
better deal	更好的價錢
better price	更好的價錢
drop the price	降點價
bargain	討價還價
a real bargain	真便宜
negotiate	討價還價
beyond my budget	超出我的預算
price is fixed	不二價
price tag	價格標籤
store-wide sale	全面大減價
big year-end sale	年終大減價

退貨

out of order	壞掉了
not work	壞了
return	退還
refund	退還，退款
compensation	賠償
exchange	退換，換貨
receipt	收據
no refund	概不退換

公共空間標語

for sale	吉屋出售
to let	吉屋出租
house for rent	吉屋招租

house for sale	吉屋出售
for rent	吉屋招租
emergency exit	太平門
lady's room	女廁所
men's room	男廁所
rest room	盥洗室
no smoking	請勿吸煙
no visitors	謝絕參觀
danger	危險
dead end	此路不通
do not touch	請勿觸摸
no admittance	閒人勿進
pull	拉
push	推
the customer is always right	顧客至上
the customer is king	顧客至上
thanks for your patronage	銘謝惠顧
thanks for coming	謝謝光臨
transaction completed	銀貨兩訖
ticket office	售票處
telephone	電話
wet paint	油漆未乾
Your browsing is welcome	歡迎光顧
Your visit is welcome	歡迎參觀
store hours	營業時間
cross walk	行人穿越道
beware of pickpockets	謹防扒手
barber shop	理髮廳

指引方向詞彙

east	東
south	南
west	西
north	北
left	左
right	右
straight on	往前直去
go straight ahead	直走
there	那兒
here	這兒
front	前方
back	後方
opposite	對面的
by	在…旁
fork	分岔
side	側旁
before	之前
after	之後
cross	橫越
between	在…中間
across from	在…對面
in front of (= before)	在…（之）前
in back of (= behind)	在…（之）後
around the corner from ...	在…的轉角
on the corner of A and B	在 A 和 B 轉角
on the main road	在主要道路上

block	街區，街廓

臉部表情／情緒

smile	微笑
smirk	假笑
snicker	竊笑，嘻嘻作笑
chuckle	輕笑
giggle	傻笑
grin	嬉笑
guffaw	狂笑，捧腹大笑
laugh	大笑
cackle	尖笑
gloat	得意，幸災樂禍
love	喜愛
amaze	驚愕
shocked	震驚
angry	憤怒
glare	怒視
roar	怒吼
snarl	怒罵
snub	斥責
cry	哭泣
moan	嗚咽
weep	哭泣
frown	皺眉
fidget	煩躁，坐立不安
panic	恐慌
surprised	驚訝

bashful	害羞
shy	害羞
cower	膽怯
cringe	畏縮
cold	冷酷
calm	平靜
ponder	沉思
boggle	猶豫
yawn	呵欠
tired	疲倦
bored	無聊
sigh	歎息
groan	呻吟
whine	牢騷
blink	眨眼
stare	盯視
curious	好奇
confuse	迷惑
thirsty	口渴
hungry	饑餓

身體動作 - 頭部

peer	偷窺
gaze	凝視
nod	點頭
listen	聆聽
see	看見
smell	聞

breathe	呼吸

身體動作 - 口部

shout	呼喊
burp	打嗝
sniff	吸氣
sneeze	打噴嚏
whistle	口哨
cheer	歡呼
cough	咳嗽
drink	喝酒
eat	進食
gasp	喘氣
lick	添舌
talk	談話
taunt	嘲弄
applaud	喝彩
sing	唱歌
spit	吐出
bite	啃咬
mourn	哀悼
whisper	耳語，私下說出，低聲說出
murmur	喃喃自語
plead	懇求
praise	讚美
scream	尖叫
speak	說話
blow	吹

身體動作 - 手部

raise	舉手
crack	響指
shrug	聳肩
dig	挖
cut	切
draw	劃(線)
nose pick	挖鼻
tap	輕拍
poke	手戳
salute	敬禮
curtsy	行禮，女子行屈膝禮
hail	致敬
shoot	射擊
wave	揮手
clap	鼓掌
surrender	投降
slap	摑…耳光
bye	再見
tickle	撓癢
scratch	抓癢
welcome	歡迎
shoo	驅趕，用"噓"聲趕走
beckon	招手
greet	問候
kiss	飛吻
point	指點

massage	按摩
lock	上鎖
open	打開
write	寫
carry	提
pull	拉
push	推
hit	打，打擊
throw	丟
touch	摸，接觸
wash	洗
wipe	擦拭
sew	縫
knit	編織
paint	繪畫
brush	刷
knock	敲
bring	攜帶
drive	開車
fix	修理

身體動作 - 腿部

beg	跪求
kneel	跪拜，跪著
kick	踢
stand	站立
grovel	曲膝，匍匐
bounce	蹦跳

jump	跳
climb	爬
crawl	爬行
walk	走路
run	跑
ride	騎
dance	舞蹈

身體動作 – 軀幹

bow	鞠躬
shiver	打顫
shake	顫抖
shimmy	擺動
apology	道歉
sit	坐下
sleep	睡覺
lay down	躺下
hug	緊擁
cuddle	擁抱
duck	閃避
dance	跳舞
fart	放屁
tease	挑逗

身體動作 – 其他

thank	感謝
threaten	恐嚇
rude	粗魯

insult	侮辱
comfort	安慰
bush	埋伏
ready	就緒
play	遊戲
congratulate	恭喜
wait	等待
stop	停止
sweep	清，掃
think	想
sleep	睡覺
read	讀書
wake	清醒
move	移動
fly	飛

常用形容詞

alert	機敏的，警覺的
witty	機智的，愛說風趣話的
shrewd	精明的，機敏的
sharp-minded	機智的
intelligent	聰明的
watchful	機敏的
smart	明的
sensible	明智的
mild	溫和的
obedient	聽話的，順從的
humble	謙恭的

careful	小心的
creative	有創意的
curious	好奇的
frank	坦白的，直率的
cheerful	歡樂的
carefree	無憂無慮的
ingenious	心靈手巧的
ingenuous	天真無邪的
naive	天真的，幼稚的
charitable	慈善的，慷慨的
benevolent	仁慈的
humane	仁慈的，人道的
compassion	同情
compassionate	有同情心的
sympathetic	有同情心的
merciful	仁慈的，寬大的
impartial	公正的
disinterested	公正的
unselfish	無私的，不謀私利的
detached	不偏不倚的，超然的
tolerant	容忍的，寬容的
genuine	真誠的，坦率的
generous	大方的，慷慨的
decent	正派的，像樣的
courteous	有禮貌的
enthusiastic	熱心的
cordial	熱誠的，友善的

warmhearted	熱心的
thoughtful	體貼的
earnest	認真的，誠摯的
despair	絕望
disappointed	失望的
frustrated	沮喪的
gloomy	抑鬱的，悲觀的
grief	悲痛，傷心
upset	傷心的
sentimental	多愁善感的
regretful	後悔的
moody	憂鬱的，不快的，易怒的
sorrowful	悲傷的
sullen	抑鬱的，沈悶的
troubled	煩惱的，不安的
melancholy	憂鬱的
down-hearted	情緒低落的
half-hearted	不認真的
anxious	憂慮的，發愁的
horrible	可怕的
dreadful	可怕的
horrify	使恐懼
frighten	驚恐，使驚恐
cowardly	膽怯的
hostile	敵意的，不友好的
indignant	憤怒的
mad	發狂的，瘋狂的

outrageous	勃然大怒的
irritating	氣人的
furious	狂怒的
quarrelsome	愛爭吵的
bad-tempered	脾氣不好的
careless	粗心大意的
thoughtless	粗心大意的
cautious	謹慎的
ignorant	無知的
ill-advised	欠考慮的，輕率的，不明智的
uninformed	無知的，不學無術的
impulsive	衝動的，莽撞的
clumsy	笨拙的
insincere	不真誠的
dishonest	不誠實的
spiteful	懷恨的，惡意的
snobbish	勢利的
malicious	懷惡意的，惡毒的
wicked	邪惡的
narrow-minded	心胸狹窄的
mischievous	調皮的，惡意的
merciless	冷酷無情的
offensive	討厭的，無禮的
rude	魯莽的
hasty	魯莽的，倉促的，草率的
scornful	輕蔑的，蔑視的

deceitful	欺詐的，不老實的
persevering	持之以恆的
persistent	堅持不懈的
superficial	膚淺的
shallow	膚淺的
showy	炫耀的
stingy	吝嗇的
sociable	愛交際的
hospitable	殷勤好客的
hearty	衷心的，熱誠的
humorous	幽默的
awkward	尷尬的，笨拙的
bias	偏心
conceited	驕傲的，自負的
conservative	保守的
daring	大膽的
dependent	依賴的
depressed	壓抑的
disobedient	不順從的
character	性格
characteristic	特性，特徵，特點
disposition	性情，性格
challenging	挑戰的
competent	有才能的
capable	有能力的
dominant	支配的，統治的

frugal	勤儉節約的
economical	節儉的
thrifty	節儉的，節約的
diligent	勤奮的
dependable	可信賴的
eccentric	古怪的
effective	有效的
efficient	效率高的
extravagant	奢侈的
fantastic	太好了
forgive	原諒
fragile	脆弱的，易碎的
hypocritical	虛偽的
impatient	不耐煩的
inactive	無生氣的，不快活的
incapable	無能的
incompetent	不勝任的
incredible	難以置信的
indifferent	漠不關心的
insistent	堅持的，顯眼的
interfere	干涉，干預
intrusive	闖入的
irresponsible	不負責任的
inspirational	鼓舞人心的
laborious	勤奮的
neglectful	疏忽的
obstinate	頑固的，固執的

odd	古怪的，奇怪的
overwhelming	壓倒的，勢不可擋的
patient	有耐心的
passionate	易動情的
pastime	消遣，娛樂
pessimistic	悲觀的
optimistic	樂觀的
pretentious	矯飾的
productive	有成效的，有收穫的
qualified	合格的
reckless	不計後果的
redundant	多餘的
reliable	可依賴的
reluctant	不願意的
reserved	拘謹的，有克制的
restrained	有節制的，拘謹的
self-controlled	鎮靜的
silent	安靜的
sincere	認真的，真心的
straightforward	正直的，老實的，簡單的
strange	奇怪的
suspicious	多疑的
talent	天才，有才能的人
temperament	氣質，稟性
trustworthy	可信任的
unconcerned	不關心的
uneasy	焦慮不安的

unintentional	無意的
unpunctual	不準時的
versatile	多才多藝的

Unit 2　吃喝玩樂篇

食物的味道

sweet	甜
salty	鹹
sour	酸
spicy	辣
too spicy	太辣了，辣死了
hot	好辣
bitter	苦
disgusting	噁心
delicious	美味的
chewy	有嚼勁的
crispy	酥脆的
crunchy	鬆脆的
rich	口味濃郁的
mushy	泥狀的
tough	硬的
juicy	多汁的
garlicky	大蒜味
light	清淡
greasy	油膩
bad tasting	難吃

上餐館

snack bar	速食店
restaurant	餐廳

make a reservation	預訂
full	客滿
all booked	客滿
How many people are in your party?	
	總共有幾位？
Party of 5!	總共有5個人！
Table for 5!	五個人的座位！
table is ready	桌子已經準備好了
smoking zone	吸煙區
non smoking zone	非吸煙區
menu	菜單
manual	菜單
order	點菜
buffet style	自助式
a la carte	照牌菜點菜
specialty	招牌菜
Today's special	今日特餐
Chef's special	主廚特餐
vegetarian	素食者
on diet	減肥或被醫師限制食物飲食
on a special meal plan	吃營養餐
drink	飲料
refill	續杯
beverage	飲料
doggy bag	把吃剩食物打包帶走
to go	外帶

for here	內用
bill	帳單
Check, Please!	買單！
separate checks	分開算
just one check	一起算
This is on me.	這次算我的。
My treat.	我請客。
go Dutch	各自付錢
cash	現金
credit card	信用卡
tip	小費
receipt	收據
thank you for coming	謝謝您的光臨

西式菜餚

smoked carp	燻鯉魚
sardine	沙丁魚
fried fish	煎魚，炸魚片
beef steak	牛排
roast beef	烤牛排
curry beef	咖哩牛排
veal cutlet, veal chop	小牛排
roast veal	烤小牛排
spiced beef	香料牛排
pork chop	豬排
roast mutton	烤羊肉
braised beef	燉牛排
lamb chop	羊排

roast turkey	烤火雞
roast chicken	烤油雞
curried chicken	咖哩雞
roast duck	烤鴨
instant noodle	泡麵
fast food	速食
spaghetti	義大利麵
pizza	比薩
macaroni	通心麵
pasta	義大利麵
lasagna	千層麵
salad	沙拉
French salad	法式沙拉醬
vegetable salad	素食沙拉
Italian	義大利式沙拉醬
ham salad	火腿沙拉
toffee	太妃糖
yogurt	優格，酸奶
Caesar Salad	凱薩沙拉
salad dressing	沙拉醬
chicken salad	雞沙拉
pickled cucumber	酸黃瓜
bread	麵包
muffin	松糕，餅
wafer	薄酥餅，威化餅
waffle	格子餅
toast	烤麵包，土司

rye bread	黑麥麵包
bun	小圓麵包
hamburger	漢堡
bacon cheeseburger	培根乳酪漢堡
French fires	炸薯條
hotdog	熱狗
sandwich	三明治
tuna sandwich	鮪魚三明治
pancake	煎餅，烤餅，薄餅
lamb chop	羊排
roast turkey	烤火雞
curried chicken	咖哩雞
pickled cabbage	泡菜
buffet	自助餐
biscuits, crackers, cookies	餅乾
chips	洋芋片，薯條
meat pie	肉餡餅，肉餡派
barley gruel	大麥粥
oatmeal	燕麥粥
blue cheese	藍帶乳酪
backed potato	烤馬鈴薯
mashed potato	馬鈴薯泥
jacket potato	烤馬鈴薯加起司等配料，帶皮煮的馬鈴薯

甜點

pudding	布丁
ice cream	霜淇淋

chocolate ice cream	巧克力霜淇淋
strawberry ice cream	草莓霜淇淋
vanilla ice cream	香草霜淇淋
ice sucker	冰棒
pie	餡餅
apple pie	蘋果派
tart	果餡餅
pastry	點心
cake	蛋糕
cream cake	奶油蛋糕
shortcake	水果酥餅
jello, jelly	果凍
yam	甜薯
sweet potato	番薯
raisin	葡萄乾

中式菜餚

sweet sour pork	糖醋肉，咕嚕肉
braised pork	紅燒扣肉
meat ball	肉丸子
sweet and sour fish	糖醋魚
Beijing roast duck	北京烤鴨
braised chicken	燜雞
steamed chicken	清蒸雞
prawn	蝦
fried prawn	炸蝦
shrimp chip	蝦片
chafting dish	火鍋

stir fried rice	炒飯
chop suey	炒雜碎，炒下水
stir fried liver	炒豬肝
bean sprouts	豆芽
tofu	豆腐
egg fried rice	蛋炒飯
congee, porridge	粥，稀飯
millet gruel	小米粥
fried pork flakes	肉鬆
lobster	龍蝦
chicken soup	雞湯
hot and sour soup	酸辣湯
steamed bun, steamed bread	饅頭
noodles	麵條
rice noodles	米粉，米線
stretched noodles	拉麵
noodles with soup	湯麵
beef noodles	牛肉麵
noodles with soybean paste	炸醬麵
fried noodles	炒麵
meat bun	包子
steamed bread with stuffing	包子
steamed twisted roll	花卷
meat pie	餡餅
pancake	煎餅，蔥油餅
dumpling	餃子
soft fried dumpling	鍋貼

wonton, dumpling soup	餛飩
sweet dumpling	湯圓，元宵
spring roll, egg roll	春捲
muffin	松糕，餅
cruller	小煎餅
deep fried dough stick	油條
soybean milk	豆漿

軟性飲料

beverage	飲料
soft drink	非酒精，軟性飲料
mineral water	礦泉水
Latte	拿鐵
Espresso	義式濃縮
Cappuccino	卡布奇諾
Caf□ Mocha	摩卡咖啡
Caf□ Aulait	咖啡歐雷
grande	大杯
tall	中杯
short	小杯
decaf	低咖啡因
low fat	低脂
non fat	無脂
decaf	低咖啡因
black coffee	黑咖啡(不加糖的咖啡)
plain coffee	純咖啡
instant coffee	即溶咖啡
white coffee	牛奶咖啡

coffee with cream and sugar

　　　　　　　　　加奶精及糖的咖啡
decaffeinated coffee　　低咖啡因的咖啡
hot chocolate　　　　　熱巧克力
tea　　　　　　　　　　茶
green tea　　　　　　　綠茶
black tea　　　　　　　紅茶
jasmine tea　　　　　　茉莉花茶
earl grey tea　　　　　伯爵茶
mint tea　　　　　　　薄荷茶
lavender tea　　　　　薰衣草茶
camomile tea　　　　　菊花茶
Assam black tea　　　阿薩姆紅茶
milk tea　　　　　　　奶茶
English breakfast tea　英式早餐茶
milk　　　　　　　　　牛奶
tea bag　　　　　　　　茶袋，茶包
fruit juice　　　　　　果汁
lemonade　　　　　　　檸檬汁
orangeade　　　　　　　橘子汁
orange juice　　　　　柳橙汁
fruit punch　　　　　　混合水果飲料
non-alcoholic cocktail　無酒精雞尾酒
cider　　　　　　　　　蘋果西打

含酒精飲料

punch　　　　　　　　潘趣酒
wine　　　　　　　　　葡萄酒

liquor	烈酒
aperitif, aperitif wine	低度酒，葡萄酒，開胃酒
white wine	白葡萄酒
red wine, port	紅葡萄酒，紅酒
Sherry	雪利酒
Martini	馬丁尼
Vermouth	苦艾酒
Whisky	威士忌
Brandy	白蘭地
Scotch	蘇格蘭威士忌
Vodka	伏特加
Gin	琴酒
Tequila	龍舌蘭酒

調酒

cocktail	雞尾酒
Pink Lady	紅粉佳人
Singapore Sling	新加坡司令
Gin Tonic	琴湯尼
Blue Moon	藍月亮
Long Island Ice Tea	長島冰茶
Side car	側車
Brandy Alexander	亞歷山大
Between the Sheets	左右逢源
Love Forgetting Water	忘情水
Brandy Eggnog	白蘭地蛋酒
Manhattan	曼哈頓

Scotch Soda	蘇格蘭蘇打
Whisky Sour	威士忌沙瓦
God Father	教父
John Collins	約翰可林
Screw Driver	螺絲起子
Bloody Mary	血腥瑪莉
Vodka Tonic	伏特加奎寧
Kamikaze	神風特攻隊
Salty Dog	鹹狗
Tequila Sunrise	日昇龍舌蘭
Margarita	瑪格麗特
Frozen Margarita	霜凍瑪格麗特
Desert's Rose	沙漠玫瑰

氣泡式無酒精飲料

carbonated beverage	碳酸飲料
Pepsi Cola, Pepsi	百事可樂
Diet Pepsi	無糖百事可樂
Diet coke	健怡可樂
cocacola, coke	可口可樂
7-up	七喜
Sprite	雪碧
soda water	蘇打水
sparkling water	蘇打水
Tonic	無糖氣泡水

氣泡式酒精飲料

| beer | 啤酒 |

light beer	淡啤酒
draught beer	生啤酒
stout beer	黑啤酒
champagne	香檳酒

蛋的煮法

sunny-side up	單煎一面的荷包蛋
scrambled egg	炒蛋
fried egg	荷包蛋
over easy	兩面煎(蛋黃半熟)
over hard	煎全熟蛋，兩面煎 (蛋黃全熟)
soft-boiled egg	半熟的水煮蛋
hard-boiled egg	煮得全熟的蛋
poached egg	蒸蛋
omelet, omelette	煎蛋捲，蛋捲

牛排的煮法

well done	全熟
medium well	稍為熟一點的
medium	適中偏生的
medium rare	三分熟的
rare	較生的

派對小點心

pizza	比薩
waffle	鬆餅
muffin	鬆糕

biscuit	餅乾
cookie	餅乾
pancake	煎餅
juice	果汁
beer	啤酒
wine	酒
cake	蛋糕
sprinkle	撒在糕點上的小糖粒
icing, frosting	糖衣，糖霜

派對相關單字

organize a party	辦派對
throw a party	辦派對
artificial flower	人造花
blindfold	蒙眼布，眼罩
streamer	彩帶
banner	寫有標語的布條
balloon	氣球
confetti	五彩碎紙
face painting	彩繪臉譜

生日派對

birthday party	生日派對
birthday cake	生日蛋糕
slumber party	睡衣派對
pajama party	睡衣派對
sleepover	

(小孩)在朋友家過夜的派對，也可單指借住在朋
友家一晚

cake	蛋糕
present	禮物
gift	禮物
wrapping paper	包裝紙
ribbon	絲帶
bow	蝴蝶結
candle	蠟燭
make a wish	許願
clown	小丑
magician	魔術師

聖誕 / 跨年派對

Christmas party	聖誕節
X'mas party	聖誕節
Christmas tree	聖誕樹
New Year's eve party	跨年派對
decorate	裝飾
ornament	裝飾品
X'mas carol	聖誕頌，聖誕歌曲
candy cane	枴杖糖
X'mas light	聖誕燈
illumination	燈會
lamp	燈泡
fireplace	火爐
reindeer	馴鹿
North Pole	北極
snowflake	雪花
celebrate	慶祝

mistletoe	槲寄生
wreath	花圈
sleigh	雪橇
Christmas lights	聖誕燈飾
star	星星
tinsel	金箔裝飾品
stocking	長襪
Bible	聖經
gingerbread man	薑餅娃娃
gingerbread house	薑餅屋
snow	雪
snowman	雪人

新生兒派對

baby shower, diaper shower, baby sprinkle
新生兒派對。在新生兒出生前,由母親及朋友
們開的派對。

diaper	尿布
pacifier	奶嘴
baby carrier	嬰兒揹袋
disposable diaper	免洗尿布
stroller	嬰兒推車
milk bottle	奶瓶
highchair	高腳椅
baby wipe	濕紙巾
crawl	爬行
bib	圍兜
teddy bear	泰迪熊

告別單身派對

bachelor party	單身派對
bachelorette party	單身女子派對
wedding shower	告別單身女子派對
bridal shower	告別單身女子派對
stripper	脫衣舞孃，脫衣舞男

結婚派對

wedding party	結婚派對
marry	結婚
wedding cake	結婚蛋糕
maid of honor	伴娘
bridesmaid	伴娘
best man	伴郎
flower girl	花童
throw a bouquet	丟捧花
bride	新娘
groom	新郎
tuxedo	燕尾服
make a toast	敬酒
propose a toast	敬酒
Congratulations!	恭禧！
tie	領帶
bow tie	蝶形領結

其他派對種類

house warming party	新居落成派對
kitchen shower	新居落成派對

farewell party	歡送會
coming of age	成年禮
superbowl party	超級盃派對
theme party	主題派對
masquerade	化裝舞會
costume party	化妝派對
poolside party	池邊派對
potluck	每人帶一道菜聚餐的派對
BBQ party	烤肉派對
tailgate party, tailgating picnic	車尾野餐會
cocktail party	雞尾酒會
banquet	酒席，筵席
buffet party	自助餐會
fashion party	時尚派對
rave party	狂歡舞會
homecoming party	

美國高中一年一度的校際舞會，多半在暑假後

prom, senior prom	舞會，畢業舞會
prom queen	舞會中評選出最美的女孩
prom king	舞會中評選出最帥的男孩
campus queen	校花
open house	

開放參觀日，在這一天所有人都可以自由前往參觀。

兒童休閒

marble	彈珠
kite	風箏
doll	娃娃
music box	音樂盒
teddy bear	玩具熊
tricycle	三輪車
puppet	木偶
robot	機器人
rocking horse	木馬
seesaw	蹺蹺板
swing	鞦韆
slide	滑梯
plastic model	塑膠
model plane	模型飛機
remote control car	遙控汽車
toy train	玩具火車
dart	飛鏢
yo-yo	溜溜球
puzzle	拼圖
windmill	風車
toy	玩具
toy bricks	積木
slingshot	彈弓
curved mirror	哈哈鏡
jump rope	跳繩
merry-go-round	旋轉木馬
pirate ship	海盜船

水上休閒活動

scuba diving	潛水
diving	潛水
snorkelling	浮潛
surfing	衝浪
wake boarding	風浪板
water skiing	滑水
jet ski	水上摩托車
parasailing	拖曳傘
catamaran sailing	雙體船
windsurfing	風帆
sailing	帆船，航行
boating	遊艇，乘船遊玩
glass bottom boat	玻璃船
rowing	划船
banana boat	香蕉船
kayak	愛斯基摩小船，獨木舟
canoeing	划獨木舟
rafting	泛舟
island hopping	列島遊
cruise	巡航，出海
dolphin cruise	出海賞海豚
sunset cruise	出海賞夕陽
night fishing	夜釣
boat hire	包船

陸上休閒活動

climbing	爬山
camping	露營
cycling	騎腳踏車
kite	風箏
fly a kite	放風箏
riding	騎馬
bungee jumping	高空彈跳

空中休閒活動

aerial excursion	空中鳥瞰
parachute	降落傘，跳傘
balloon	熱氣球
helicopter	直昇機
glide	乘滑翔機飛行
glider, hang-glider	滑翔翼，滑翔機

運動休閒

snooker, billiard	撞球
ping-pong, table-tennis	乒乓球
badminton	羽毛球
volleyball	排球
cricket	板球
squash	壁球
tennis	網球
baseball	棒球
softball	壘球

handball	手球
hockey	曲棍球
bowling	保齡球
golf	高爾夫球
snooker	英式古典撞球
billiard	美式的花式撞球
football	足球，美式足球
rugby	英式橄欖球
soccer	英式足球
basketball	籃球
swim	游泳
breaststroke	蛙式
backstroke	仰式
freestyle	自由式
butterfly stroke	蝶式
roller skating	滑輪
inline skating	溜直排輪
skating	滑冰
skiing	滑雪
ski board	滑雪板
boxing	拳擊
karate	空手道

藝文休閒

board game	棋藝，下棋
play chess	下棋
Weiqi, the game of go	圍棋
chess	象棋

bridge	橋牌
cultural show	文化表演
live band music	樂團演奏
movie	電影欣賞
theater	戲劇
symphony	交響樂
classical music	古典音樂
solo	獨奏，獨唱
choir	合唱團，唱詩班
gallery	畫廊，美術館
exhibition	展覽
landscape	風景畫
still life	靜物畫
wash	淡水彩畫
brush drawing	毛筆畫
nude	裸體畫
Chinese painting	國畫
oil painting	油畫
watercolor	水彩畫
pastel drawing	蠟筆畫
miniature	細密畫
engraving	版畫
portrait	畫像
self-portrait	自畫像
sculptor	雕塑學，雕刻
statue	人像，雕像
figure	塑像
bronze	銅像，青銅

artist	大師，藝術家
painter	畫家
author	作者
sculptor	雕刻家
artisan	工匠

健身房休閒

gymnasium, fitness room	健身房
warm up	暖身
exercise	運動，鍛鍊
work out	運動
walking	走路
jogging	慢跑
swimming	游泳
biking	騎腳踏車
push-up	伏地挺身
sit-up	仰臥起坐
weightlifting	舉重
aerobics	有氧舞蹈
step aerobic	階梯有氧

健身房設施 / 運動用品

fitness equipment	健身器材
multi-function home gym	多功能運動器材
treadmill	跑步機
exercise bike , fitness cycle	室內健身腳踏車
spin bike	飛輪健身車
rowing machine	划艇機

strength training bench	運動用長椅
tension training equipment	擴胸器
steppers	踏步機
moon walker	漫步機
elliptical trainer	運動橢圓機，登山機
pressure training equipment	壓力棒
bending bar	彎曲棒
bending spring	彎曲彈簧器
finger bar	手握器
combined training equipment	多功能拉力器
beauty salon	美容沙龍
sauna	三溫暖
steam bath	蒸氣浴
steam room	蒸氣房
health spa	健康 SPA

室內休閒

discotheque	迪斯可舞廳
karaoke	卡啦 OK
ballroom dancing	社交舞，舞廳舞
American smooth	美國式的社交舞
Modern dance	摩登舞
Latin dance	拉丁舞
Rumba	倫巴
Cha-cha-cha	恰恰恰
Samba	森巴，桑巴
Paso Double	鬥牛舞

Jive	捷舞，牛仔舞
Rock'n Roll dance	搖滾舞
folk dance	土風舞
belly dance	肚皮舞
flamengo	佛朗明哥
Mambo	曼波
Bolero	波麗露舞曲
Two-Step	兩步舞
Hustle	哈斯爾
Salsa	莎爾莎舞，騷莎
Argentine Tango	阿根廷探戈
belly dance	肚皮舞
aerobics	有氧舞蹈

賭場

blackjack	21 點
dealer	莊家
co-bank	合作坐莊
player	玩家
split	牌
pocket card	底牌
club	梅花
diamond	方塊
heart	紅心
spade	黑桃
one pair	一對
two pairs	兩對
three of a kind	三同號，或稱三條

straight	順子，或稱蛇
flush	同花，或簡稱花
full house	滿堂紅，或稱葫蘆，俘虜
four of a kind	四同號，或稱四條，鐵枝
straight flush	同花順
royal flush	大同花順
ace	A 牌
super jackpot	超級大獎
scratch card	刮刮卡
small or big	賭大小
slot	老虎機
wheel	輪盤
roulette wheel	輪盤
bluff	虛張聲勢
wild card	萬能牌
sitting out	旁觀
straight bet	直注
split bet	分注
place bet	下注
double down	加倍下注
surrender	投降認賠
shuffle	洗牌
resuffle	重新洗牌
a deck	一付牌
Roll the dice.	擲骰子吧
Let's play cards!	來玩撲克牌吧
Please don't cheat.	請不要作弊

a higher poker hand.	拿較大的牌
Change, please.	請換籌碼
Chips, please.	請換籌碼
The player wins.	玩家贏
The deck is shuffled	洗好牌了
Please place your bet.	請下注
I am totally out of luck.	我運氣真的太差了
You are lucky tonight.	你今晚真幸運

Unit 3　交通工具篇

一般交通工具

bicycle, bike	腳踏車
tricycle	三輪腳踏車
motorcycle	摩托車
motor tricycle	三輪摩托車
three-wheeler	三輪摩托車
sedan	轎車
two-door sedan	兩門轎車
four-door sedan	四門轎車
subcompact sedan	小型轎車
compact sedan	中型轎車
full-size sedan	大型轎車
hatchback	掀背式汽車
convertible	敞篷車，跑車，轎車
limo, limousine□	豪華轎車
coupe	雙門小轎車
sports car	跑車
race	賽車
car	汽車
van	箱型車
minivan	小型轎車
wagon	卡車
SUV, sport utility vehicle	運動休旅車
RV, recreational vehicle	野營休旅車

motor home	活動房屋旅行車
station wagon	客貨兩用旅行車
shooting brake	客貨兩用旅行車
truck	卡車, 旅行車
trailer	拖車
pickup truck	小貨車(無車蓋)，貨卡
light lorry, lorry	小貨車(英式)
platform truck	平臺卡車
eighteen-wheeler	18輪大卡車
heavy lorry, heavy truck	重型卡車
jeep	吉普車

公務車

ambulance	救護車
fire truck	消防車
squad car	警車，巡警車
patrol car	巡邏車
flashing lights	警示燈
siren	警鈴□
ladder	梯子
hose	水管

陸上載客交通工具

bus	公共汽車
motor coach, coach	長途客車
double-deck bus	雙層公共汽車
minibus	小巴
shuttle bus	短程交通車

taxi, cab	計程車
coach, car	火車車廂
train	火車
passenger train	載客火車
freight train	運貨列車
goods train	運貨列車
subway, underground	地下鐵
tube	地下鐵(英)

水上交通工具

ship	船
jet boat	噴射艇
vessel	船舶
cargo vessel	貨輪
cargo carrier	貨輪
cargo boat	貨輪
freighter	貨輪

空中交通工具

plane	飛機
airplane	飛機
helicopter	直昇機
chopper	直昇機
copter	直昇機
jet	噴射機
jet plane	噴射機
shuttle	太空梭
aerospace plane	太空梭，太空船
space ship	太空船

汽車零件及內裝

bumper	保險桿
chassis	底盤
fender	擋泥板
hood	引擎蓋
engine	引擎
piston	活塞
tire	輪胎
thread	輪胎花紋
cylinder	汽缸
carburetor	汽化劑
coolant	冷凍劑
lubrication	潤滑油
signal	燈號
blinker	方向燈
signal light	方向燈
headlight	車頭燈
high beam light	遠光燈
taillight	尾燈
tail lamp	尾燈
brake light	煞車燈
windshield wiper	雨刷
windshield	擋風玻璃
sun visor	遮陽板
plate	車牌
license plate	汽車牌照
exhaust pipe	排氣管

rear door	後門
rear window	後車窗
side mirror	側視鏡
rear view mirror	後視鏡
trunk	行李箱
spare tire	備胎
steering wheel	方向盤
seat belt	安全帶
seat belt buckle	安全帶扣環
A/C	空調
dashboard	儀錶版
odometer	里程表
speedometer	速度表
gauge	油表
accelerator	油門
brake	剎車
emergency brake	手剎車
clutch	離合器
gears	排檔
gear shift	排檔
automatic	自排
stick shift	手排

交通標誌

exit	高速公路出口
entrance	高速公路入口
diverted traffic	交叉路口
right junction	右交叉口

traffic circle	圓環
look right	向右看
pedestrian crossing	當心行人
signal ahead	注意號誌
construction	道路施工
no entry	禁止進入
no through traffic	禁止通行
no through way	禁止通行
do not enter	禁止進入
no left turn	禁止左轉
no right turn	禁止右轉
no U-turn	禁止迴車
no bicycles	禁行自行車
no honking	禁按喇叭
no loitering	禁止逗留
no parking	不准停車
no stops	不准停留
do not stop	請勿逗留
no stopping at any time	任何時間不准停車
pedestrian crossing	前有人行道
please drive carefully	請小心駕駛
road closed	此路封閉
slow	慢行
speed limit of xxx	限速每小時 XXX
VIP car park	貴賓停車場
guest's car park	來客停車場
limited parking	停車位有限

parking lot	停車場
parking area	停車場
car park	停車場
parking permitted	允許停車
no parking	禁止停車
parking for taxis only	只准許出租停
please do not park	請不要停車
strictly no parking	嚴禁停車
hill	險降坡
slippery	路滑
merge	匝道會車
one way	單行道
two-way traffic	雙向道
detour	繞道行駛
stop	停

陸上公共運輸常用詞彙

waiting room	候車室
platform	月臺
express train	快車
track, rail	鐵軌
slow train	慢車
subway station	地鐵車站
get off, get on	下/上車
conductor	售票員
stop	車站
station	車站
traffic jam	交通擁擠

berth	臥舖
roomette	臥舖
seat	座位
hard sleeper	硬臥
soft sleeper	軟臥
bus stop	車站
bus terminal	終點站

海上公共運輸常用詞彙

ferry	渡輪
pier	碼頭
on boat	船上
in port	(船)靠岸
lounge	休息室
cabin	甲板
upper deck	上層甲板

空中公共運輸常用詞彙

check in	登機手續
passport	護照
ticket	機票
window seat	靠窗座位
aisle seat	走道座位
middle seat	中間的座位
non smoking seat	非吸煙區的座位
emergency exit	緊急出口
legroom	伸腳的空間
toilet	洗手間

lavatory	洗手間
economy class	經濟艙
first class	頭等艙
business class	商務艙
on schedule	準點
boarding pass	登機證
luggage claim slip	行李認領單
gate	登機門
boarding gate	登機口
connecting flight counter	轉機櫃檯
scale	(行李)磅秤
carry-on item	隨身行李
check your luggage	行李託運
terminal A	A 航站
confirm the flight	確認航班
make a flight reservation	預定機票
pre-boarding announcement	登機前的廣播
stewardess	女乘務員
steward	男乘務員
flight attendant	空服員
fasten the seat belt	繫上安全帶
pilot	駕駛員
customs officer	海關官員
passenger	乘客
take off	起飛
departure time	起飛時間
arrival time	飛抵時間
destination	目的地

大眾運輸常用詞語

time table	車時刻表
return ticket	回程票
one way ticket	單程票
book a ticket	訂票
refund	退票
transfer	換車
change	換車
information desk	問訊處
delay	誤點
fare	票價
exact change	恕不找零

車站機場港口常見標語

Keep your belongings with you at all times.
隨時注意你的物品。

These seats are meant for elderly and handi-
capped person & women with children.
博愛座（供老人，殘疾人及攜有兒童的婦女）。

Do not speak to the driver.
請勿與司機交談。

Bus lane	公共汽車道
Bus stand	公共汽車停車處
Bus information	公共汽車詢問處
Please keep gateways clear	請保持通道暢通
Stand clear off the door	請勿站在門口

Please retain your ticket for inspection.

請保留車票待驗。

tourist service	觀光局服務台
tourist service center	觀光局服務中心
information	詢問處
taxi loading	計程車上客處
taxi stand	計程車候車處
Toilet engaged	廁所有人
Mind the gap	小心月臺階間隙
Ticket valid until xxx.	車票有效期到 xxx。
bus loading	上車處
passenger terminal	航站大廈
money exchange	外幣兌換處
post office	郵局
airport lounge	機場休息室
arrival	入境
arrival lobby	入境大廳
arrival parking lot	入境停車場
departure	出境
departure parking lot	出境停車場
departure waiting lounge	出境休息廳
transit lounge	過境室
entry and exit service	入出境服務站
exit, out	出口
entrance, in	入口
holding room	候機室
check in area (zone)	辦理登機區

customer lounge	旅客休息室
flight connections	轉機處
domestic flights	國內航班
passport control	入境檢驗
emergency exit	安全出口
exit	出口

Please leave your luggage with you at all times.
請隨身攜帶你的行李。

airport shuttle	機場班車
queue here	在此排隊
help desk	詢問處
no smoking	禁止吸煙
left baggage	行李寄放
lost property	失物招領
Luggage pick up	取行李
Luggage reclaim	取行李
baggage claim	提領行李
reclaim belt	取行李傳送帶
baggage cart	行李推車
check-in counter	旅客登機報到台
customs information	海關服務台
customs service	海關服務台
payment of customs duty	海關課稅處
quarantine	檢疫
duty free shop	免稅商店
gift shop	禮品店
restaurant	餐廳

snack bar	快餐冷飲
flight kitchen	空中廚房
aviation medical center	航空醫療中心

Unit 4　美容保養篇

體型及外貌

physique	體格，體型，多談男人的身材
figure	身材，多談女人的身材
muscular	肌肉發達
curvy figure	曲線玲瓏
stacked	曲線玲瓏
big	個頭很大
small	個頭小
beer belly	啤酒肚
overweight	超重的
fat	肥胖的
baby fat	嬰兒肥
chubby	豐滿，胖嘟嘟
thin	瘦瘦的
skinny	瘦的
slim	苗條
tall	高的
thin	瘦的
short	矮的
slender	修長苗條的
good-looking	好看的
handsome	英俊的
pretty	漂亮
cute	可愛的

ugly	醜的
beautiful	美麗的
attractive	有吸引力的
charming	迷人的
heavy	重的
pretty	漂亮的

保養品名稱常見字首

acne	青春痘用品
spot	青春痘用品
clean-	清潔用
purify-	清潔用
hydra-	保濕用
anti-	抗、防
alcohol-free	無酒精
multi-	多元

保養品的作用

solvent	溶解
repair	修護
revitalize	活化
nutritious	滋養
gentle	溫和的
anti-wrinkle	抗老防皺
balancing	平衡酸鹼

保養清潔用品外觀

| foam | 泡沫式 |

milk	乳狀
cream	霜狀
gel	膠狀，透明

膚質分類

oily	油性膚質
dry	乾性膚質
normal	中性膚質
combination	混合性膚質
sensitive	敏感型膚質

皮膚清潔用品

face wash	洗面乳
facial cleanser	臉部清潔
remover	卸妝露
makeup remover	卸裝水
makeup removing lotion	卸裝乳

皮膚深層清潔用品

deep cleanser	深層清潔
pore cleanser	毛孔清潔
pore refining	毛孔潔淨
nose cleansing strip	

妙鼻貼，一種用於清潔鼻頭粉刺的貼布

| exfoliate | 去角質 |
| scrub | 磨砂膏 |

皮膚基礎保養品

| toner | 化妝水，爽膚水 |

astringent	收斂水
freshener	化妝水
gentle tonic	溫和化妝水
firming lotion	緊膚水
lotion	化妝水，凝露
smoothing tone	柔膚水
essence	精華液
moisturizer	保濕
cream	霜
moisturizer cream	護膚霜
day cream	日霜
night cream	晚霜
eye gel	眼部保養凝膠
lip balm	護唇膏
lip care	護唇用
facial mist	臉部保濕噴霧
facial spray	臉部保濕噴霧
complexion mist	臉部保濕噴霧

皮膚加強保養

eye mask	眼膜
mask	面膜
facial mask, masque	面膜
pack	美容塗敷劑，面膜
peeling	剝落式面膜
facial	作臉
lymphatic drainage	淋巴引流排毒

頭髮保養

shampoo	洗髮精
hair conditioner	潤髮乳
hair dressing gel	護髮乳
treatment	護髮乳
hair pack	護髮膜
hot oil	熱油保養

手／腳指甲保養

manicure	指甲，修指甲
nail saver	護甲液
manicure	修指甲
pedicure	足部護理
hand lotion	護手霜
hand moisturizer	護手霜

身體保養

body wash	沐浴精
body shampoo	沐浴精
body lotion	身體潤膚露
body moisturizer	身體保濕
exfoliate	去角質(身體或臉)
scrub	磨砂膏(身體或臉)

身體防曬

sun block	防曬用品
sun screen	防曬用品
tanning lotion	助曬劑

dark tan oil	助曬油
after sun	日曬後用品
whitening	美白
tan	曬成棕色
bronze	曬黑，古銅色
skin bronzed	皮膚曬黑
self tanning room	沙龍的助曬機，不用外出曬太陽也可以曬的很均勻。

身體除毛

hair removal	除毛
depilate	脫毛
shaving	刮除毛髮
waxing	熱蠟除毛
tweeze	以鉗子拔除毛髮
laser hair removal	雷射除毛
ingrown hair	毛髮內生

（以拔除方式除毛者可能會產生這樣的問題）。

bikini line	比基尼線

（穿比基尼時會露出體毛的部分，通常在夏天時會將之剔除）。

bikini waxing	比基尼線除毛
Brazilian waxing	比基尼線除毛，巴西式
eyebrow shaping	修眉
hairy	多毛的，毛茸茸的
body hair	體毛
armpit hair	掖毛
lip hair	嘴唇上的細毛

belly hair	肚臍下的毛
leg hair	腿毛，腳毛
pubic hair	陰毛

減肥

diet, dieting□	節食
slim	減肥
weight	體重
overweight	過重
weight loss	減重
obesity	肥胖
goal weight	目標體重

減肥方式

diet pill	減肥藥
diet entree	減肥餐
meal replacement	代餐
artificial sweetener	代糖
physical activity	運動
fitness	健身
weight loss surgery	減肥手術
bariatrics surgery	減肥手術
obesity surgery	減肥手術

減肥評估

nutritionist	營養師
dietitian	營養師
energy imbalance	熱量失衡

recommended dietary allowance	
	建議飲食容許
nutritional value	營養價值
nutritional status assessment	營養情況評估
diet	飲食，膳食
high fiber diet	高纖維飲食
low cholesterol diet	低膽固醇飲食
reducing diet	減肥飲食
therapeutic diet	治療性飲食
low fat diet	低脂飲食
BMI, body-mass-index	身體質量指數
BIA, bio-electrical impedance	體脂肪
BMR, basal metabolic rate	基礎代謝率
waist circumference	腰圍
WHR, waist-hip ratio	腰臀比□
underweight	過輕
malnutrition	營養失調

食物中的成分

vitamin	維生素
anti-haemorrhagic vitamin	抗出血維生素
fat-soluble vitamin	脂溶性維生素
water-soluble vitamin	水溶性維生素
vitamin A	維生素 A
vitamin B12	維生素 B12
vitamin B6	維生素 B6
vitamin C	維生素 C
vitamin D	維生素 D

vitamin E	維生素 E
folic acid	葉酸
mineral	礦物質
phosphorus	磷
potassium	鉀
sodium	鈉
sulphur	硫磺
manganese	錳
magnesium	鎂
iodine	碘
iron	鐵
chlorine	氯
cobalt	鈷
copper	銅
calcium	鈣
fluorine	氟
caloric	熱量的，卡路里的
fat	脂肪
calorie	卡路里
carbohydrate	碳水化合物，醣
starch	澱粉
sucrose	蔗糖
fatty acid	脂肪酸
fructose	果糖
galactose	半乳糖
glucose	葡萄糖
nutrition	營養

protein	蛋白質
carotene	胡蘿蔔素
roughage	粗食的
cellulose	植物纖維素
dietary fibers	食物纖維
lactic acid	乳酸
lactose	乳糖
lipid	脂質
lipoprotein	脂蛋白
triglyceride	三酸甘油脂
cholesterol	膽固醇
low-calorie	低卡
low-carb	低碳水化合物
low-fat	低脂

彩妝打底

make up base	妝前霜，飾底乳，隔離霜
foundation	隔離霜，粉底
liquid foundation	粉底液，通常較服貼。

stick, pan-stick foundation
粉條，條狀粉底，通常質地偏乾，遮瑕力也較好。
2-way cake, powder fundation
兩用粉餅，可乾濕兩用的粉餅

mousse foundation	慕絲狀粉底
concealer	遮瑕膏
pressed powder	粉餅

lucidity	蜜粉
loose powder	蜜粉
powder	粉底，蜜粉

彩妝眼部

eyeliner	眼線，眼線筆
liquid eye liner	眼線液
eye shadow	眼影
mascara	睫毛膏
false eye lash	假睫毛
brow powder	眉粉
brow pencil	眉筆
waterproof	防水

彩妝修容

shading powder	修容餅
blush	腮紅
color blush	腮紅
shimmering powder	亮粉
glitter	亮片

唇部彩妝

lip gloss	唇彩
lip color	口紅
lip liner	唇筆
lipstick	口紅
long last lipstick	持久性口紅
lip coat	口紅保護膜

臉部彩妝／保養工具

cosmetic applicator	彩妝工具
cosmetic accessory	彩妝工具
applicator	刷具
pencil sharpener	削筆器
brush	刷子
eye brush	眼影刷
lash curler	睫毛夾
electric lash curler	燙睫毛器，睫毛電卷器
brow brush	眉刷
brow template	畫眉器
blush brush	腮紅刷
lip brush	口紅刷
puff	粉撲
sponge	海綿
facial tissue	面紙
Kleenex	可麗舒，面紙

（原為品牌名稱延伸而為面紙通稱）

tissue	面紙
oil absorbing sheet	吸油面紙
cotton pad	化妝棉
cotton bud	棉花棒，棉籤
Q-tip	棉花棒，棉籤

（原為品牌名稱延伸而為棉花棒通稱）

shaver	刮刀
razor	刮鬍刀

electric shaver 電動刮毛刀

指甲保養工具

nail care 護甲油
nail color 指甲油
nail enamel 亮光指甲油
nail polish 亮光指甲油
top coat 表層護甲液
nail polish remover 去光水
pedicure 足部指甲，修趾甲
manicure 修指甲
quick dry 快乾

頭髮造型

perm 燙髮
dye hair 染髮
perm hair 燙髮
trim 修剪
thin 打薄
layer 打層次
cut 剪髮
hairdo (女子)髮式，髮型
hairstyle 髮型
crop 平頭
crew cut 平頭
flattop 平頭
part 分邊，分髮
forehead 前額

hairline	臉際線
bang	瀏海
fringe	短瀏海
short hair	短髮
long hair	長髮
medium long hair	中長髮
curly	捲髮
wavy bouncy	微捲
soft wave	自然大波浪捲髮
straight	直髮
ponytail	馬尾
afro	米粉頭
bob	齊耳短髮
braid	辮子
pigtail	辮子
bun	髮髻

頭髮造型工具

hairdresser	美髮師
hairdressing	理髮業
styling gel	造型髮膠
mousse	慕絲，造型用泡沫
roll	髮捲
roller	捲髮器
perm roller	捲髮器
crimper	捲髮器
clippers	電推剪
perm formula	冷燙劑

cold waving lotion	冷燙劑
hairdryer	吹風機
hairgrip	小髮夾
clip	夾子
clamp	鯊魚夾
hairpin	髮簪
snood	網狀帽，束髮用的繩狀帶子
hairnet	髮網

各種美容整型手術

cosmetic surgery	美容整形手術
plastic aesthetic surgery	美容整形外科手術
plastic surgery	美容整形外科手術
plastic surgeon	整形外科醫生
ops, operations	手術
collagen	膠原蛋白
botox; botulinum toxin	肉毒桿菌
hyaluronic acid	玻尿酸，簡稱 HA
Restylane, Hylaform	玻尿酸(品牌名稱)
placenta extract	胎盤素
liposuction	抽脂
breast reconstruction	乳房重建
breast augmentation	乳房增大術
breast reduction	乳房縮小術
breast deformity	乳房矯正術
breast surgery	隆胸手術
breast implant	隆胸

breast enlargement	隆胸
silicon	矽膠
saline bag	生理食鹽水袋
eyelid surgery	割雙眼皮
augmentation rhinoplasty	隆鼻
rhinoplasty	整鼻手術
nose job	隆鼻
butt implants	豐臀
jaw implant	隆下巴
bellybutton surgery	肚臍美容
vaginal reconstruction	陰道重建手術
scar revision	除疤痕
nevus	除痣
mole	痣
laser treatment	雷射美容治療
dermabrasion	磨皮
facelift	拉皮
micro facelift	局部拉皮

其他整型相關單字

self-esteem	自信
carry out	完成，執行
celeb	藝人，名人
celebrity	藝人，名人
vanity	虛榮心
go under the knife	動手術
put pressure on	使...感到壓力
iron out	燙平

natural looks	天生樣貌
abnormal	不正常的
artificial	人工
de-wrinkled	消除皺紋
fake	假的

名牌採購相關單字

| boutique | 精品店 |

monogram
(將姓名的首字母組成的)組合圖案，例如：LV
圖案的經典提包款就叫做 monogram

dust bag	防塵袋
designer	設計家，服裝設計師，
	設計名家

手提包類

wallet	皮夾
purse	女用手提包
shoulder bag	有肩帶的皮包
briefcase	公事包
backpack	登山包，背包
suitcase	小提箱
trunk	大衣箱

女鞋類

dress shoes	精緻鞋，時裝鞋
high-heeled shoes	高跟鞋
Mary Janes	有扣帶的低跟女鞋
boots	靴，長統靴

bootee	輕巧女靴
fashion boots	時尚靴
thigh boots	統高至大腿之靴子
knee boots	長統靴
half boots	中統靴
high cut	高統
mid cut	中統
low cut	低統
chukka boots	高及足踝的高統鞋
ankle boots	短靴，足踝靴

運動鞋類

sport footwear	運動鞋類
athletic shoes	運動鞋
casual shoes	便鞋
jogging shoes	慢跑鞋
basketball shoes	籃球鞋
hiking boots	健行靴
tourist shoes, travel shoes	旅遊鞋
racing shoes	跑鞋
flaty shoes	平底便鞋
sneakers	膠底帆布運動鞋

露趾式鞋款

slippers	拖鞋
flip-flops	人字拖鞋
felt shoes	毛氈鞋
paper slipper	紙拖鞋

sadal	涼鞋
zori	夾趾涼鞋，日式便鞋，草鞋
stripy sandal	多帶式涼鞋

特殊用途鞋款

crampon	釘鞋(冰上行走)
sabot	木鞋
work footwear	工作鞋
custom shoes	定製鞋
embroidery shoes	繡花鞋
roller skate shoes	溜冰鞋
skiing shoes	滑雪鞋
skating shoes	滑冰鞋
jockey boots	騎馬用鞋
ballet shoes	芭蕾舞鞋
fishing wader	釣魚鞋
orthopaedic shoes	矯正鞋

鞋子的設計

shoe designer	鞋樣設計師
shoemaker	鞋匠
latest design	最新的款式
footwear	鞋類
point toe	尖形鞋頭
oval toe	橢圓形鞋頭
round toe	圓形鞋頭
square toe	方形鞋頭
peep toe shoes	露趾尖式

too hard	太硬
too soft	太軟
trimmings	飾物
children shoes	童鞋
men's shoes	男鞋
ladies' shoes	淑女鞋
high heels	高跟鞋
leather shoes	皮鞋

鞋子的相關零件

sole	鞋底
heels	鞋跟
foot pad	鞋墊
lace	鞋帶
tip	前套，鞋跟尖
toe	鞋頭
toe cap	鞋頭
tongue	鞋舌
Velcro	魔術帶黏扣帶
shoe horn	鞋拔

男女裝種類

suit	西裝，套裝
shirt	襯衫
double-breasted jacket	雙排扣西裝
single breasted	單排扣
double breasted	雙排扣
tie	領帶

tie-pin	領帶夾
vest	背心
tailcoat	燕尾服
pants	褲子
trousers	西褲(英)
short pants	西短褲
overalls	背帶褲，工作褲
slacks	寬鬆的長褲
socks	襪子
scarf	領巾，圍巾
trench coat	風衣
cape	披風
overcoat	大衣
working wear	工作服

女裝種類

evening dress	晚禮服
blouse	(女)襯衫
dress	(女)洋裝
vest	背心
skirt	裙子
slim skirt	窄裙
pantyhose	褲襪

香水的種類(由濃至淡)

perfume	濃香水，香料
essence de perfume	香精性香水
eau de parfum	香水，香氛(濃度較香精低)

eau de toilette   淡香水(濃度較香水低)
eau de cologne
古龍水(濃度較淡香水低,多為男性香水)
eau de fraicheur
清香水(香水濃度最低,多為體香劑或鬍後水)

香水相關字

wear	擦(香水)
apply	用(香水)
fragrance	香水
cologne	古龍水
aftershave	鬍後水(一種刮鬍後用的香水)
scent	氣味
subtle	輕微的,不知不覺的
strong	強烈的

配件類

hairpin	釵
headgear	頭飾
dangler	耳環,晃來晃去的東西
earbob	耳飾,耳環
earring	耳飾
tongue ring	舌環,晃來晃去的東西
tongue bar	裝在舌頭上
ring	戒指
finger ring	戒指

necklace	項鏈
pendant	項鏈的墜子
brooch	胸針
bracelet	手鏈
tennis bracelet	由塊狀物連接起來的手鏈
brace lace	手鏈
navel jewelry	肚臍飾品
belly ring	環狀肚臍飾品
dangle	有墜子的肚臍飾品
bangle	手鐲，腳鐲
toe ring	戴在腳趾上的戒指

金銀珠寶詞彙

jewelry shop	珠寶店
diamond	鑽石
genuine diamond	真鑽
CZ diamond	水鑽
crystal	水晶
crystal glass	水晶玻璃
rock crystal	水晶
rubasse	紅水晶
amethyst	紫水晶
acicular crystal	髮晶
karat	K金
platinum	鉑，白金
plating	鍍金
gold plated	鍍金
genuine gold	真金，赤金

gold bar	金條
gold filled	包金
ornamental gold	飾金
covered silver	鍍銀的
pure silver	純銀的
silver ornament	銀飾
sterling silver	標準純銀，純銀
gem	寶石，寶物
gemstone	寶石
ruby	紅寶石
garnet	石榴石，夜明珠 深色 紅寶石
sapphire	藍寶石
topaz	黃寶石，黃玉，托帕石
synthetic cut stone	人造寶石
amber	琥珀
jade	玉，玉石
jadeite	硬玉，翡翠
emerald	翡翠，祖母綠
jasper	碧玉
alexandrite	紫翠玉
ivory	象牙
olivine	橄欖石
opal	貓眼石，蛋白石
cloisonn□	景泰藍的
enamel	琺瑯
agate	瑪瑙

coral	珊瑚
pearl	珍珠
rosee	桃色珍珠
colored pearl	有色珍珠
natural pearl	天然珍珠
fresh water pearl	淡水珍珠
genuine pearl	珍珠
olivet	人造珍珠
orient	上等珍珠
shell	貝殼

Unit 5 身體保健篇

人生各時期

fetal stage	胎兒期
ovi-germ stage	胚卵期
embryo stage	胚胎期
neonatal period	新生兒期
term infant	足月兒
premature	早產兒
post term infant	過期產兒
perinatal stage	圍產期，出生前後時期
infancy	嬰兒期
baby	嬰兒
little baby	幼嬰
infant	嬰兒
childhood	童年期
toddler age	幼兒期
preschool age	學齡前
school age	學齡期
kid	兒童
child	兒童
little child	幼童
prepuberty	青春早期
puberty	發育期，青春期
adolescence	青春期(指 puberty 至 adulthood 之間的過程。)

prepubescence	青春前期
postpubescence	青春後期
boy	男孩
little boy	小男孩
girl	女孩
little girl	小女孩
youngster	小孩，年輕人
young man	小夥子
youth	青少年
teenager	青少年
juvenile	青少年
adolescent	青少年，青春期的孩子
maturity	成人期
adulthood	成人期
adult	成人
grown-up	成人的
man	男人
men	男人(複數)
woman	女人
women	女人(複數)
manhood	男性成年期
womanhood	女性成年期
menopause	更年期
old age	老年期
old	老的
aged	老的
elderly	上了年紀的

in years	老年
at a good old age	老年期
senile	老態龍鍾的

成長發育常用字

growth	生長
development	發育
maturity	成熟
physical development	身體發育
sexual prematurity	性早熟
masturbation	手淫
spermatorrhea	夢遺
menarche age	月經初潮年齡
delayed puberty	性發育延遲
contraceptive	避孕藥
birth control	避孕
secondary sex characters	第二性徵
nutrition	營養
malnutrition	營養不良
endocrine	內分泌
insufficiency of intake	攝入不足

外傷處理

wound	傷口
unintentional injury	意外傷害
external wound	外傷
wound management	傷口護理
wound margin	傷口周邊

wound depth	傷口深度
sterilization	消毒
infection	感染
discolored	變色的(指傷口附近皮膚)
color	(傷口)顏色
swell	(傷口)腫脹
edema	(傷口)水腫
exudate	滲出物，組織液
tissue	組織
brown necrotic tissue	棕色壞死組
slough	腐肉
granulation	肉芽(形成)
blood stain	血污
purulent	化膿的
bleeding	流血的，出血的
bleeding badly	留了很多血
the volume of bleeding	出血量
odor	味道(異味)
inflamed	發炎的

皮膚的感覺

itch	癢
itchy	癢癢的
itching	發癢
tingling	刺刺的
pain	痛
painful	痛痛的

hurt	痛
touch	觸覺
burn	灼傷
dry	(傷口周圍)乾乾的

形容痛覺

ache, pain	痛
no pain	不會痛
not pain	不會痛
mild pain	一點點痛
slight pain	輕微的痛
moderate pain	有點痛
severe pain	很痛，嚴重疼痛
acute pain	劇痛，急性疼痛
intermittent pain	一陣一陣的痛
pain come at intervals	間歇性的痛
constant pain	持續的痛
continuous pain	持續的痛
persistent pain	持續性痛
(feel pain) at dressing change	
	換藥時才會痛
tingling pain	刺痛
prickling pain	刺痛
piercing pain	刺骨的痛
throbbing pain	抽痛
sharp pain	急劇的痛，刺痛
dull pain	鈍痛，暗痛

pressing pain	按壓時會痛
burning pain	灼痛
tearing pain	撕裂般疼痛
sore pain	腫痛
crushing pain	壓迫痛
ache all over	全身疼痛
colic	絞痛
cramping pain	絞痛
crampy pain	痙攣痛
distended pain	脹痛
radiating pain	擴散痛
stabbing pain	刀刺痛
sore pain	潰爛痛

身體疾病／症狀 - 四肢及骨骼

stiffness in shoulder	肩膀僵硬
back pain	背痛
scoliosis	脊椎側彎，脊柱側凸
lordosis	脊椎側彎，脊柱前凸
kyphosis	脊椎側彎，脊柱後凸，駝背
low back pain	腰痛
sprain	扭傷
graze	擦傷，抓破
dislocation	脫臼
fracture	骨折
cramp	抽筋，痙攣
bruise	淤傷，淤青

trauma	外傷
scratch	擦傷，抓傷
scrape	擦傷
twist	扭傷
cut	割傷
handicapped	殘癈

身體疾病／症狀 － 胸腔

chest pain	胸痛
pneumonia	肺炎
heart disease	心臟病
heart attach	心臟病發作
myocardial infraction	心肌梗塞
heart failure	心臟衰弱
congenital heart disease	先天性心臟疾病
arteriosclerosis	動脈硬化症
angina	狹心症
cardiac neurosis	心臟神經症
cardiac asthma	心臟喘息
myocarditis	心肌炎
endocarditic	心內膜炎
valvular cyanosis	心臟瓣膜疾病
arrhythmia	心律不整
pleurisy	胸膜炎
bronchitis	支氣管炎
bronchial asthma	支氣管氣喘
pulmonary	肺氣腫
respiratory system	呼吸系統

difficulty in breathing	呼吸困難
expiration	呼氣
inspiration	吸氣
bradycardia	心搏徐緩
short of breath	不能呼吸

身體疾病 / 症狀 – 頭部及耳鼻喉

fever	發燒
high fever	高燒
headache	頭痛
migraine	偏頭痛
earache	耳痛
deaf	**聾**
sore throat	喉嚨痛
stuffy nose	鼻塞
runny nose	流鼻涕
asthma	哮喘，氣喘
wheezing	哮喘
tinnitus	耳鳴
sneeze	打噴嚏
cough	咳嗽
dry cough	乾咳
moist cough	有痰咳
hemoptysis	咳血
blood-spitting	吐血
pharyngitis	咽頭炎
huskiness	聲音沙啞
hoarseness	沙啞

sputum	痰
snore	打鼾
hiccup	打嗝

身體疾病 / 症狀 - 眼睛

astigmatism	散光
myopia	近視
nearsightedness	視
hyperopia	遠視
farsightedness	遠視
color blindness	色盲
trachoma	沙眼
cataract	白內障
blind	盲

身體疾病 / 症狀 - 口腔疾病

gingivitis	牙齦炎
toothache	牙齒痛
periodontosis	牙周病
plaque	牙菌斑
fill	補牙
decay	蛀牙
cavity	齲齒
caries	齲齒
bad breath	口臭
lip crack	嘴唇乾裂

身體疾病 / 症狀 - 傳染病

acute infectious diseases	急性傳染病
flu	流感
influenza	流感
infectious diseases	傳染病
cold	感冒，傷風，著涼
dysentery	痢疾
tetanus	破傷風
cholera	霍亂
malaria	瘧疾
scarlet fever	猩紅熱
mumps	流行性腮腺炎
smallpox	天花
syphilis	梅毒
tetanus	破傷風
rabies	狂犬病
bronchitis	支氣管炎
diphtheria	白喉
pneumonia	肺炎
typhus	斑疹傷寒
measles	麻疹
German measles	德國麻疹
hay fever	花粉症
T.B., tuberculosis	肺結核
pulmonary tuberculosis	肺結核
phthisis	癆病，肺結核
chicken pox	水痘

身體疾病／症狀 – 腹腔疾病 (肝膽腸胃脾腎)

abdominal pain	腹痛
abdominal enlargement	腹部膨脹
digestive system	消化系統
appendicitis	盲腸炎
stomachache	胃痛，也可引申為腹痛
gastritis	胃炎
gastritis ulcer	胃潰瘍
nephritis	腎炎
hyperacidity	胃酸過多症
indigestion	消化不良
diarrhea	腹瀉
loose stool	軟便
bloody stool	血便
mucous stool	粘液便
bloody urine	血尿
cloudy urine	尿混濁
pyuria	膿尿
constipation	便秘
hepatitis	肝炎
cirrhosis of the liver	肝硬化
appendicitis	闌尾炎
peritonitis	腹膜炎
intestinal tuberculosis	腸結核
rumbling sound	腸鳴

intestinal catarrh	腸黏膜炎
colitis	大腸炎
duodenal ulcer	十二指腸潰瘍
volvulus	腸扭結
cholecystitis	膽炎
gall stone	膽結石症
jaundice	黃疸
pancreatitis	胰臟炎
pass gas	放屁
fart	放屁
anorexia	食慾不振
intussusception	腸套腸
ascariasis	蛔蟲病

身體疾病 / 症狀 - 心理疾病

neurasthenia	神經衰弱
epilepsy	癲癇
insanity	精神病
insomnia	失眠症

身體疾病 / 症狀 - 女性相關

anemia	貧血
pregnancy	懷孕
conceive	懷孕
labor pain	分娩陣痛
period	月經
menstrual pain	經痛
miscarriage	流產

abortion	流產

身體疾病／症狀 － 皮膚

skin disease	皮膚病
sunburn	太陽灼傷
burn	燙傷，燒傷
acne	痘痘
freckle	雀斑
pimple	面皰，暗瘡
mole	痣
birthmark, nevus	胎記，痣
dermatitis	皮膚炎
contact dermatitis	接觸性皮膚炎
scaly skin	鱗狀皮
eczema	濕疹
infantile eczema	小兒濕疹
seborrhea eczema	脂漏性濕疹
measles	麻疹
urticaria	蕁麻疹，風疹塊
drug eruption	藥疹
rash	疹
red rash	紅疹
roseola	玫瑰疹
tinea	癬
psoriasis	牛皮癬
scabies	疥
frost bite	凍瘡
scalding	燙傷

lupus	狼瘡
corn	雞眼
athletes foot	香港腳
wart	疣
boil	瘡
gangrene	壞疽

身體疾病 / 症狀 - 腫瘤

cancer	癌
tumor	腫瘤
in situ carcinoma	原位癌
invasive cancer	侵襲癌
nasopharyngeal carcinoma	鼻咽癌
thyroid cancer	甲狀腺癌
cancer of the oral cavity	口腔癌
skin cancer	皮膚癌
leukemia	白血病
rectal cancer	直腸癌
cancer of the colon and rectum	結直腸癌
esophagus cancer	食道癌
stomach cancer	胃癌
gastric cancer	胃癌
intestine cancer	小腸癌
liver cancer	肝癌
lung cancer	肺癌
bladder cancer	膀胱癌
breast cancer	乳癌
cancer of the womb	子宮體癌

cervical cancer	子宮頸癌
prostate cancer	攝護腺癌
radiation pain	放射痛

身體疾病 / 症狀 - 其他

disease	疾病
uncomfortable	不舒服
body odor	狐臭，體臭
heat stroke	中暑
poisoning	中毒
endemic	水土不服
stupor	昏迷
coma	昏迷狀態
shock	休克
allergy	過敏
faint	暈倒
difficulty in swallowing	吞嚥困難
inflammation	發炎
ulcer	潰瘍
neuralgia	神經痛
paralysis	麻痺
poliomyelitis	脊髓灰質炎
diabetes	糖尿病
rheumatism	風濕病
arthritis	關節炎
stroke	中風
hemiplegia	半身不遂
septicemia	敗血病

hypertension	高血壓
hypotension	低血壓
anemic	貧血的
palpitation	心悸
thrombosis	血栓症
aneurysm	動脈瘤
anus fistula	瘻管，痔瘻
hemorrhoids, piles	痔瘡
sense of pressure	壓迫感
hunger pain	飢餓痛
nausea	噁心
vomit	嘔吐
shuddering	發抖
chill	打冷顫，畏寒
night sweat	盜汗
sweat	發汗
pale	臉色發白
pallor of face	顏面蒼白
asthenia	虛弱
fatigue	疲勞
cyanosis	青紫
tiredness	倦怠
obesity	肥胖症
heat exhaustion	輕度中暑，熱衰竭
heat stroke	中暑
asthma	哮喘
electric shock	觸電
injury	受傷

bleeding　　　　　　　　　出血

醫院各處室

hospital	醫院
clinic	診所
admitting office	住院處
registration office	掛號處
waiting room	候診室
consulting room	診室
outpatient	門診病人
outpatient department	門診部
inpatient	住院病人
inpatient department	住院部
outpatient surgical center	門診手術中心，一般小手術
ER; Emergency Room	急診室
OR; Operation Room	手術室
nursing department	護理站
labor and delivery room	接生房
medical office	醫務所
medical clinic	醫務室
pharmacy, dispensary	藥房，領藥處
laboratory	實驗室，病菌培養及化驗
mortuary	太平間，停屍間
morgue	太平間，停屍間
blood bank	血庫
records department	病歷室
standard room	普通病房

ward　　　　　　　　病房
medical ward　　　　　　內科病房
surgical ward　　　　　　外科病房
pediatric ward　　　　　　小兒科病房
CCU; Coronary Care Unit
心臟科護理病房
ICU; Intensive Care Unit
加護病房，深切治療室
MICU; Medical Intensive Care Unit
內科加護病房
SICU; Surgical Intensive Care Unit
外科加護病房
PICU; Pediatric Intensive Care Unit
小兒科加護病房
NICU; Neonatal Intensive Care Unit
新生兒加護病房
Speech Therapy Unit
語言治療部
ECU; Extended Care Unit
延續護理部
Home Care, Long Term Care Unit
家庭護理部
TCU; Terminal Care Unit　末
期護理部
hospice and palliative care
安寧病房，末期患者病房
recovery room

恢復室
rehabilitation center
康復中心
Physiotherapy Department
物理治療部
Public Health Unit
公共衛生中心
Radiotherapy Unit　放攝治療部
Occupational Therapy Department
職業治療部

醫院門診類別

Department of Traditional Chinese medicine

中醫科

acupuncture	針灸
Internal Medicine	內科
surgical department	外科，手術
Cerebral Surgery	腦外科
Ophthalmology	眼科
Optometry	驗光科

Otolaryngology, (ENT; ears, nose and throat)

耳鼻喉科

Inhalation Therapy	呼吸治療科
Allergy and Immunology	過敏性專科
Orthodontics	牙齒矯正科
Dentistry	牙科
Cardiology	心臟科
Cardio Surgery	心臟外科

Pulmonary Medicine	肺科
Chiropractic	脊椎神經科
Neurology	神經科
Neurosurgery	神經外科
Gastroenterology	腸胃科
Nephrology	腎臟科
Colorectal Surgery	結腸直腸外科
Urology	泌尿科
Endocrinology	內分泌科
Obstetrics, Gynecology	婦產科
Podiatry	足科
Geriatrics	老人病專科
Hematology	血液科
Infectious Disease	傳染病科
Family Practice	家庭醫學科
Pediatrics	小兒科
Dermatology	皮膚科
Skin Department	皮膚科
Plastic surgery	整形外科
Radiology	放射科
X-ray department	X光放射科
Radiation Oncology	癌症放射科
Pathology	病理科
Psychiatry	精神治療科
Physiatrics	復健科
Orthopedic surgery	整形外科
Vascular Surgery	血管外科

Orthopedic Surgery	骨科手術
Orthopedic	骨科
Osteopathy	整骨療科
Anesthesiology	麻醉科
Oncology	癌症專科

醫院相關人員

Doctor	醫生
Nurse	護士
Social work	社工
Physician	內科醫生
Physician's Assistant	醫生助手
Medical Assistant	醫務助理
Genetic Counselor	遺傳病輔導員
Psychologist	心理醫師，心理學家
Nurse Midwife	接生護士
Midwife	助產士
Psychological Counselor	心理輔導員
Therapist	心理醫師
Shrink	心理醫師
Physical Therapist	復健師，物理治療師
Audiologist	聽力訓練專家
Respiratory Therapist	呼吸治療員
Dentist	牙醫
Dental Assistant	牙醫助理
Dietitian	營養師
Nutritionist	營養專家
Laboratory Technician	化驗師

Pharmacologist	藥理學專家
Pharmacist	藥劑師
Health Technician	健康技員
Medical Technologist	醫學技師
X-Ray Technician	X光科技員
Home Visiting Nurse	家訪護士
health care professional	醫療專業人員

醫學檢查常見詞彙

prescription	處方
diagnose	診斷
clinic	診所
symptom	症狀
treatment	治療
examination	檢查
general check-up	健康診斷
physical examination	健康診斷
ECG, electrocardiogram	心電圖
mammography	乳房攝影
vaginal laparoscope	陰道鏡
cervical smear	子宮頸抹片
smear	抹片
biopsy	切片檢查
national health insurance	全民健保
prevention	預防
build	體格
blood	血液
blood type	血型

tuberculin reaction	結核反應
congenital	先天性病
relative	親戚
heredity	遺傳
immunity	免疫
diagnosis	診斷
quarantine	檢疫，隔離
suspected	疑似
affect	感染
infection	感染
epidemic	流行性的
incubation	潛伏期
virus	濾過性病毒
disorder	失調
chronic	慢性的
acute	急症，急性的
pulse rate, pulsation	脈搏數
rapid pulse	快脈
irregular pulse	不規則脈
respiration rate	呼吸數
breath, respiration	呼吸
death rate	死亡率
crude cancer incidence rate	癌症粗發生率
chronic diseases	慢性疾病
red cell	紅血球
white cell	白血球
bowel movement	排便

blood analysis	驗血
blood test	驗血
Celsius, centigrade	攝氏
Fahrenheit	華式
thermometer	體溫計
stool	便
loose stool	軟便
bloody stool	血便
mucous stool	粘液便
clay-colored stool	粘土樣便
urine	尿
bloody urine	血尿
cloudy urine	尿混濁
pyuria	膿尿
glycosuria	糖尿
relapse	復發症
casualty	急症
serous	血清的
confirmed	確認的
offensive	刺激性的
admission to hospital	入院
discharge from hospital	退院
clinical history	病歷
blood pressure	血壓

醫學治療詞彙

resection	切除
prescription	藥方

operation	手術
irrigation	沖洗
enema	灌腸
serum	血清
anesthesia	麻醉
local anesthesia	局部麻醉
general anesthesia	麻醉全身
intravenous anesthesia	靜脈麻醉
spinal anesthesia	脊椎麻醉
vaccinate	注射疫苗，種牛痘
injection	打針，注射
I.V., intravenous drip	點滴
aromatherapy	芳香治療法
massage	推拿
chiropractic	整脊
side effect	副作用
ultrared ray	紅外線
infrared ray	紅外線
UV; ultraviolet ray	紫外線

身體部位 - 骨骼

bone	骨
skeleton	骨骼
spinal marrow	脊髓
spine, vertebra	脊椎
backbone	脊骨，脊柱
skull	顱骨，頭蓋骨
cheek bone	顴骨

collarbone	鎖骨
rib	肋骨
breastbone	胸骨
joint	關節
pelvis	骨盆

身體部位 - 肌肉／血管／神經

muscle	肌肉
sinew	腱
organ	器官
blood vessel	血管
vein	靜脈
artery	動脈
capillary	毛細血管
nerve	神經
lymph	淋巴腺
circulatory system	循環系統

身體部位 - 口腔

tooth	牙齒
denture	假齒
dental crown	牙冠
gum	牙齦
incisor	門齒
molar	臼齒，大牙
wisdom tooth	智齒
milk tooth	乳齒
deciduous teeth	乳牙

permanent teeth	恆牙
tongue	舌頭
oral cavity	口腔
oral epithelium	口腔上皮
epithelium	上皮
mouth floor	口底
saliva	唾液(口水)
dribble	流口水
drool	流口水
palate	顎
masticatory muscle	咬合肌肉

身體部位 - 頭部

head	頭
brain	腦
hair	頭髮
bald head	禿頭
baldness	禿頭
dry	乾燥，乾枯髮質
split	分岔
damage	受損髮質
brittleness	易斷裂
breakage	受損
split ends	分叉

身體部位 - 臉部

| skin | 皮膚 |
| face | 臉 |

forehead	額頭
eye brow	眉毛
eye	眼
lid	眼瞼
nose	鼻子
nose ridge	鼻樑
nostril	鼻孔
temple	太陽穴
cheek	臉頰
dimple	酒窩
mouth	嘴
lip	嘴唇
chin	下巴
beard	山羊鬍
full beard	大鬍子
whisker	落腮鬍
mustache	小鬍子
goatee	山羊鬍子
tile beard	瓦形鬍
military moustache	軍人鬍
stubble beard	殘鬚，鬍渣
sideburns	鬢角
ear	耳

身體部位 - 肩頸部

neck	脖子
throat	咽喉

tonsil	扁桃腺
wrinkle	皺紋
windpipe	氣管
bronchus	支氣管
shoulder	肩

身體部位 － 胸部

diaphragm	隔膜
chest	胸部
gullet	食道
esophagus	食道
heart	心臟
atrium	心房
ventricle	心室
lung	肺
breast	乳房
nipple	乳頭
papilla	乳頭
tit	乳頭
areola	乳暈

身體部位 － 腰腹部

navel, belly button	肚臍
abdomen	腹部
waist	腰
gall	膽囊
gall bladder	膽囊
kidney	腎臟

liver	肝臟
pancreas	胰腺
spleen	脾
stomach	胃
bladder	膀胱
small intestine	小腸
large intestine	大腸
duodenum	十二指腸
appendix	盲腸
rectum	直腸

身體部位 - 男 / 女性徵

penis	陰莖
testicle	睪丸
testis	睪丸
balls	陰囊(口語)
peanut	男性生殖器官(口語)
scrotum	陰囊
urine	尿道
ovary	卵巢
uterus, womb	子宮
vagina	陰道
pubic hair	陰毛
axillary hair	腋毛
armpit hair	腋毛

身體部位 - 背 / 臀部

back	背
hip	臀部
breech	臀
buttocks	屁股
bottom	屁股
anus	肛門

身體部位 - 四肢

extremities	四肢
trunk	軀幹
thumb	大拇指
forefinger	食指
index finger	食指
middle finger	中指
ring finger	無名指
little finger	小指
pinkie	小指
palm	手掌
nail	指甲
fist	拳頭
knuckle	指關節
back	手背
wrist	手腕
elbow	肘
armpit	腋下
foot	腳
instep	腳背
toe	腳趾

ankle	踝
heel	腳後跟
sole	腳底
arch	腳掌心
thigh	大腿
kneecap	膝蓋骨
knee	膝蓋
shank	小腿
calf	小腿肚

藥品名稱

pain killer	止痛藥(針)
ointment	軟膏
eye medicine	眼藥
medicine, drug	藥
tablet, pill	藥丸
capsule	膠囊
cough medicine	止咳藥
sublingual tablet	舌下錠
aspirin	阿斯匹靈
suppository	栓劑
antibiotic	抗生素
medicine	藥品
enema	灌腸劑
drug	藥
toxic	有毒
toxicant	毒品
heroin	海洛因
morphine	嗎啡

quietive 鎮靜劑

醫療用具

ice bag 冰袋
scissors 剪刀
thermometer 體溫計
bandage 繃帶
adhesive tape 膠帶

更多醫療用品請見日用品篇 之 生活用具 - 急救箱

急救常識

EAR, expired air resuscitation

吹氣法人工呼吸
mouth-to-mouth 口對口
mouth-to-nose 口對鼻
mouth-to-mouth and nose 口對口鼻
ECC, external chest compression

心臟外壓法
CPR, cardiopulmonary resuscitation

心肺復甦術

Unit 6　校園單字篇

學校裡的職稱

Chancellor, President	大學校長
Dean	學院的院長
Assistant Professor	助教授
Associate Professor	副教授
Head of the faculty	系主任
Head of the division	部門主任
Chairman	主席
Faculty	全體教授
Teaching Assistant	助理
Professor	教授
Lecturer	講師
Counselor	輔導老師
Principal	中學校長
Headmaster	小學校長
Headmistress	小學女校長
Teacher	老師

學校裡其他人稱

student	學生
guest student	旁聽生
Alma Mater	母校
alumnus	男校友，校友
alumni	alumnus 的複數
alumna	女校友

181

alumnae	女校友(複數)
postgraduate	研究生
freshman	大一新生
sophomore	指大二學生
junior	指大三學生
senior	指大四學生

課程申請

application	申請
applicant	申請者
application form	申請表
on-line application	線上申請表
application for enrollment	註冊申請表
international student details	國際學生資料
course selection	欲申請之課程
program name	欲申請之課程名稱
prerequisite	先修課程

學雜費

tuition	學費
living expense	生活費
applicant's payment information	申請人付費資訊
money order	匯票
check	支票
cardholder	持卡人
waiver	減免
application fee	申請費
application fee waiver request	申請手續費減免

tuition waiver	學費減免
assistantship	給研究生的一種經濟資助
deposit	押金
enrollment deposit	註冊訂金，以保留位置
express mail charge	快遞費
loan	助學貸款
payable to	支票的收款人
bursar	學校之財務及會計部門

就學其間常見詞彙

letter of recommendation	推薦信
appraiser	推薦者
confidential	機密
seal	密封
referee	推薦人
reference	推薦信
recommendation	推薦信
capacity	關係，用在推薦信中
coeducation	男女生同校制度
boarding school	寄宿學校
private school	私立學校
public school	公立學校
orientation	新生訓練
scholarship	獎學金
class	課程，班級
lecture	課程
enroll	報到
enroll	註冊

matriculation	大學入學許可
tuition fee	學費
miscellaneous expenses	雜費
term	學期
commencement date	課程開課日期
closed date	課程結束日期
attendance date	就學時間
transfer	轉學生
special student	特殊學生
transfer student	插班生申請為轉學生
audit	旁聽，
(沒有學分或考試，費用與正式生相同)	
exchange student applicant	
	交換學生申請者
full-time student	全職學生
part-time student	兼職學生
work-study	半公半讀從事校內工作的學生
semester	學期
trimester	學期
term	學期
quarter	學期
register	登記，註冊
major	主修
minor	輔修
double major	雙修
joint degree	雙修學位

mandatory	必修
elective	選修
mandatory course	必修課
credit	學分
unit	學分
courses planned	預計要修的課程
courses in progress	現在正在修的課程
courses current enrolled	現在正在修的課程
non-exam subject	不考試的科目
curriculum	課程安排
Syllabus	

一整個學期的課程進度，在每學期開始時由教授發給學生參考。

reading homework	閱讀功課
recitation	小組討論
lecture	課，課程
workshop	實習課
lab	實習
schedule, school timetable	課表
cut school	翹課，曠課
drop school	輟學
drop out	輟學，退學
quit school, expel from school	開除，退學
dismiss from school	退學
withdraw	退選(一門課)
drop	退選一門課
grade	年級別

| dismissed | 退學處分 |
| detention | 留校察看 |

學校宿舍

standard room	標準房
en-suite room	含衛浴的套房
bedding requirement	寢具需求
bedding pack	套裝寢具
duvet	棉被，鴨絨墊子
pillow	枕頭
sheet	床單
duvet & pillow case	被套及枕頭套
moving out	搬離(寢室)
summer vacation room	暑期宿舍

作業及考試

essay	短文
thesis	論文
paper	論文
dissertation	論文
exam	考試
pop test	隨堂測驗
pop quiz	小考
open book exam	開書考試，可以參考書帶入考場
midterm	期中考
final	期末考
final exam	期末考

oral test	口試
transcript	成績單
report card	成績單
flunk	不及格
study plan	讀書計畫
statement of purpose	讀書計畫

留學考試

TOEFL; Test of English as a Foreign Language
托福考試

IELTS; International English Language Testing System
雅思測驗

GEPT; General English Proficiency Test
全民英檢

Placement Test
入學前的程度測驗，通常是英文考試。

ACT; American College Test
就是美國大學入學測驗，一般做為美國各大學申請入學的參考條件之一

SAT; Scholastic Assessment Test
由美國大學委員會(The College Board，大約 3900 所大學共同組成的文教組織)主辦，是美國學生進入大學的一種測驗。

GMAT; Graduate Management Admission Test
由美國教育測驗服務社(Educational Testing Services，簡稱 ETS)舉辦，作為商學研究所申請入學條件之一。

GRE; Graduate Record Examinations

同樣由美國教育測驗服務社（ETS）舉辦，為
美國各大學研究所或研究機構的申請入學參考
條件之一。

MCAT; Medical College Admission Test

為美國醫學院入學測驗，是學校評估申請入學
者未來在醫(藥)學院是否有足夠能力學習課程的
參考條件之一。

LSAT; Law School Admission Test

由美國法律測驗服務社(Law Services)定期在世
界各地舉辦，做為美國法學院的申請入學參考
條件之一。

教育學制

academic year　　　　　　學年

early childhood education

兒童教育，多指五歲以下兒童的學齡前教育

day care center　　　　　　托兒所

family day care　　　　　　家庭托兒所

nursery school　　　　　　托兒所

preschool　　　　　　　　學前班

kindergarten　　　　　　　幼稚園

elementary education

初等教育六年(屬於12年義務教育)

elementary school　　　　國小

primary school　　　　　　國小

secondary education

中等教育六年(屬於12年義務教育)

intermediate program,
junior high school   中級教育三年
secondary program, high school

    二等教育三年
senior high school   高中
higher education   高等教育
adult education   成人教育
community and junior college

    兩年制大學
community college   社區大學
two-year college   兩年制學院
undergraduate   四年制大學
University   大學
College   學院，大學的統稱
Professional school   專業學校
Graduate school   研究所

畢業學位

graduation ceremony   畢業典禮
commencement   畢業典禮
diploma   文憑，畢業證書
graduation certificate   畢業證書，文憑
degree   學位
Bachelor   學士
Master   碩士
Doctor of Philosophy   博士
Associate Degree   副學士學位
A.A. ; Associate of Arts   文副學士

A.S. ; Associate of Science	理副學士
Bachelor Degree	學士學位
BA; Bachelor of Arts	文學士
BS; Bachelor of Science	理學士
First Professional Degree	初級專業學位
MD; Doctor of Medicine	醫學士
JD; Juries Doctor	法學士
Master Degree	碩士學位
MA; Master of Arts	文學碩士
MS; Master of Science	科學碩士
MBA; Master of Business Administration	
	企管碩士
M.F.A.; Master of Fine Arts	藝術碩士
LL.M.; Master of Law	法學碩士
MED; Master of Education	教育碩士
Doctoral Degree	博士學位
Ph.D.; Doctor of Philosophy	哲學博士
J.S.D.; Doctor of Judicial Science	
	法學博士
D.Ed./Ed.D.; Doctor of Education	
	教育博士
D.Sc./Sc.D.; Doctor of Science	
	科學博士

數理學科

math, mathematics	數學
algebra	代數
geometry	幾何

science	科學，理科
biology	生物
chemistry	化學
biochemistry	生物化學
physics	物理
medicine	醫學
physical geography	地球科學
astronomy	天文學
metallurgy	冶金學
atomic energy	原子能學
chemical engineering	化學工程
engineering	工程學
mechanical engineering	機械工程學
electronic engineering	電子工程學

文學科

Chinese	中文
English	英語
Japanese	日語
history	歷史
geography	地理
literature	文學
linguistics	語言學
library	圖書館學
diplomacy	外交
foreign language	外文
mass-communication	大眾傳播學
journalism	新聞學

商學科

commercial science	商學
economics	經濟學
politics	政治學
banking	銀行學
accounting	會計學
finance	財政學
accounting and statistics	會計統計
business administration	工商管理

其他學科

anthropology	人類學
sociology	社會學
social science	社會科學
psychology	心理學
philosophy	哲學
civil engineering	土木工程
architecture	建築學
law, jurisprudence	法學
botany	植物
zoology	動物學
agriculture	農學
gymnastics	體育

Unit 7　報刊新聞篇

相關人員

contributing editor	特約編輯
accredited journalist	特派記者
stringer	特約記者，通訊員
correspondent	駐外記者，常駐外埠記者
journalist	新聞記者
cameraman	攝影記者
reporter	記者
columnist	專欄作家
free lancer	自由撰稿人，自由業者
contributor	投稿人
editor	編輯
copy editor	文字編輯
proofreader	校對員
PR, public relation	公關(人員)
remuneration	稿費，薪資
publisher	出版者

新聞採訪製作編輯

journalism	新聞業，新聞學
fourth estate	第四等級(新聞界的別稱)
copy desk	新聞編輯部，編輯者用的辦公桌

editorial office	編輯部
wire service	通訊社
news agency	通訊社
publishing house	出版社
censor	審查稿件，新聞審查
morgue	報刊資料室
nation-wide	全國性的
nat'l, national	全國的
around the world	國際新聞版
entertainment	娛樂版
tourism	旅遊專版
financial section	報刊的金融版
domestic news	國內新聞
stocks	股市版
lifestyle	生活版
focus	新聞聚焦
banner	橫幅標題
layout	版面編排
makeup	版面設計
full position	醒目位置
blank	開天窗，新聞內容不足
faxed photo	傳真照片
caption	圖片說明
crop	剪輯(圖片)
cut	插圖，字數刪減
cut line	插圖說明
boil	壓縮篇幅

gutter	中縫
dateline	新聞上註名的時間地點
byline	署名文章
deadline	截稿時間
five "W's" of news	新聞五要素
insert	插稿
file	發稿
filler	補白
stone	拼版
trim	刪稿件
kill	退稿
reject	退稿
spike	退稿
inverted pyramid	倒金字塔的寫作結構
subscribe	訂購
circulation	發行量
issue	發行

一般常用字

carry	刊登
daily	日報
weekly	週報
monthly	月刊
bi-monthly	雙月刊
quarterly	季刊
periodical	期刊
journal	期刊
newspaper	報紙

evening paper	晚報
morning paper	晨報
popular paper	大眾化報紙
quality paper	內容較嚴肅的報紙
digest	文摘
magazine	雜誌
tabloid	小報，以報導聳動話題為主
clipping	剪報
column	專欄，欄目
interview	專訪
feature	特寫，專稿
newsprint	新聞紙
medium	媒體，媒介
media	媒介，媒體(複數)
mass communication	大眾傳播學
mass media	大眾傳播媒介
editorial	社論
editor's notes	編者按，總編摘記
supplement	副刊，增刊
flag	報頭，報名
master head	報頭，報名
headline	新聞標題，內容提要
top news	頭條新聞
front page	頭條
red-hot news	最新消息

subhead	小標題，副標題
lead	導語，導讀
highlights	要聞
brief	簡訊
bulletin	新聞簡報
documents	文獻
story	消息，文章，稿件
thumbnail	短文，略圖
essay	隨筆
round-up	綜合消息
readability	可讀性
hot news	熱點新聞
hard news	硬新聞，純消息
soft news	軟新聞
scandal	醜聞
reader's interest	讀者興趣
assignment	採訪任務
beat	採訪範圍
cover	採訪
dig	深入採訪，深入追蹤，挖掘新聞
exclusive	獨家新聞
exclusive interview	獨家採訪
scoop	搶到獨家，獨家新聞
covert coverage	隱性採訪，秘密採訪
the grapevine	小道消息
unconfirmed report	未經證實的消息

hearsay	小道消息
back alley news	小道消息
sources close to...	接近…的人士消息
it is said…	據說
it is reported…	據報導
it is learned…	據悉
it is understood…	據瞭解
reports say…	據報導
rumors say…	據謠傳
attribution	消息出處，消息來源
source	新聞來源，消息來源，可靠人士
reliable source	消息可靠人士
well-informed source	消息靈通人士
well-placed source	重要消息人士
authoritative source	權威人士
authorities	權威人士(複數)
authoritative information	官方消息
government statement	政府聲明
the quarters concerned	有關方面
official source	官方人士
government official	政府官員
highly-placed source	高層消息來源
diplomatic source	外交人士
police source	警方人士
military source	軍方人士
advance	預發消息，預寫消息

tip	透露(秘密消息或內幕)
pipeline	匿名消息來源
according to an anonymous source	
	據匿名消息來源說
insider	內部人士
in-group source	圈內人士
observers	觀察家
analysts	分析家
a source who asked not to be identified (or disclosed)	據不願透露姓名人士指出
unimpeachable source	可靠消息人士
off the record	不宜公開報導，私下的
extra	號外
expose	新聞曝光，揭發
freedom of the press	新聞自由
watchdog	輿論監督
opinion poll	民意測驗
snap poll	即席調查
questionnaire	調查表
press	報刊，新聞界
press conference	記者會
news conference	記者招待會
press release	新聞稿
press law	新聞法
press corps	記者團

press briefing	新聞發表會
news briefing	新聞發表會
document released by...	由…所發佈的消息
update	更新(新聞內容)
timeliness	時效性,時新性
nose for news	新聞敏感,新聞鼻
objectivity	客觀性
slant	主觀報導,片面報導
sensational	聳人聽聞的,具有轟動效應的
background	新聞背景
news clue	新聞線索
news peg	新聞線索
news value	新聞價值
informative	見聞廣博的

寫事件

pseudo event	假新聞
invasion of privacy	侵犯隱私權
libel	誹謗罪
suspended interest	懷疑,懸疑
eye-account	目擊記,記者見聞
skeleton in the closet	見不得人的秘密
Achilles' heel	(唯一的)致命傷,弱點
intangible cultural heritage	無形的文化遺產
air crash	飛機失事
chute, parachute	降落傘

copter, helicopter	直升機
chopper	直升機
frame-up	誣陷，陷害
flying squad	機動小組
crash, collision	碰撞，墜毀
public opinion	輿論
imported red fire ant	入侵紅火蟻
flay	批評
rap	批評
rebuke	批評
criticize	批評
insult	侮辱
separation	隔離，分離
quarantine	隔離
clash	發生分歧，爭議
curb	控制
check, examine	檢查，拷問(口語)
grill, investigate	調查
probe	調查
plot, conspire	預謀，密謀策劃

寫人物

profile	人物特寫，人物專訪
man of mark	名人，要人
man of the year	年度風雲人物
come out	出櫃，承認是同性戀
come out of the closet	出櫃，承認是同性戀
homosexual	同性戀的正式說法

homo	同性戀
gay	男同性戀
queer, fairy, queen	男同性戀，較輕蔑的說法
lesbian	女同性戀
heterosexism	異性戀主義者
gay liberation	同性戀解放運動
women's liberation	婦女解放運動
campaign against porns	
	掃黃運動
enlisted man	現役軍人
big gun	有勢力的人，名人

國際要聞 / 政治新聞

foreign radios announced	
	據外電報導
foreign wire services were cited as saying	
	援引外國通訊社的消息說
It is authoritatively learned	
	自權威方面獲悉
coup plotter	政變策劃者
dictatorship	獨裁
one-man government	獨裁政府
appropriate authority	有關當局
peace saboteur	和平破壞者
interim government	過渡政府
bloodless coup	不流血政變
hostage	人質
curfew	宵禁，戒嚴

dusk-to-dawn curfew	徹夜宵禁
blockade	封鎖
vacuum	淨空
apartheid	種族隔離
racial discrimination	種族歧視
blast	爆炸
explosion, explode	爆炸
abortive coup attempt	政變未遂
ballistic missile	彈道導彈
ballistic missile test	彈道導彈試驗
ABM; anti-ballistic missile	反彈道導彈
ground-to-air missile	對空導彈
long-range nuclear missile	遠程核導彈
SALT; Strategic Arms Limitation Talks	
	限制戰略武器會談
SDI; Strategic Defense Initiative	
	戰略防禦措施
atomic nucleus	原子核
nuclear weapon	核子武器
atomic weapon	原子武器
denuclearization	(使國家或地區)
	非核化
armed intervention	武裝干涉
rout	擊潰，打垮
oust, expel	驅逐
raid, attack	進攻
head, direct	率領

gut, destroy	摧毀
nip, defeat	擊敗
pullout, withdrawal	撤退，撤離
strife, conflict	衝突，矛盾
feud	嚴重分歧，長期爭鬥，世仇
dispute	嚴重分歧
row, quarrel	爭論，爭議
clash, controversy	爭議
lift an embargo	解除禁運
embargo	禁運，封港
all-out ban	全面禁止
mull, consider	考慮
weigh	考慮
balk	阻礙
impede	阻礙
foil	阻止，防止
nix	否決，拒絕
vote down	否決
ban	禁止
prohibit, forbid	禁止
bar, prevent	防止，阻止
lib	解放
liberation	解放
UNESCO; United Nations Educational, Scientific And Cultural Organization	聯合國教科文組織

permanent member	常任理事國
allied powers	同盟國
axis powers	軸心國
face-to-face talk	會晤
top-level talk	高峰會談
arm-twisting	施加壓力
peaceful co-existence	和平共處
peace-keeping force	維和部隊
amicable relations	友好關係
21-gun salute	21響禮炮
red carpet welcome	隆重歡迎
honor guard	儀隊
guest of honor	貴賓
reciprocal visit	互訪
strategic petroleum reserve	戰略石油儲備
crude output	原油生產
crude oil	原油

APEC; Asia-Pacific Economic Cooperation
亞太經合組織
ASEAN; Association Of Southeast Asian
Nations
東南亞國家聯盟，東盟
OAU; Organization Of African Unity
非洲統一組織
PLO; Palestine Liberation Organization
巴勒斯坦解放組織，巴解
OPEC; Organization Of Petroleum Exporting
Countries
石油輸出國組織

205

WHO; World Health Organization
世界衛生組織
WTO; World Trade Organization
世界貿易組織
GATT; General Agreement
On Tariffs And Trade
關貿總協定
IOC; International Olympic
Committee
國際奧林匹克委員會
IMF; International Monetary Fund
國際貨幣基金組織
amendment　修正案，附加條款
NASA; National Aeronautics
And Space Administration
美國國家航空暨太空總署
Pentagon
五角大樓，美國國防部
DP; Democratic Party
美國民主黨
GOP; Grand Old Party
美國共和黨
Dems; Democrat
民主主義者，民主人士，美國民主黨黨員
Republican　　　美國共和黨黨員
Duma　　　　　俄羅斯國會
bombard　　　　轟炸，炮擊

truce	停火，休戰
ceasefire	停火
pact	條約
agreement, treaty	條約，協議
deal, agreement	協定
fair-trade agreement	互惠貿易協定
transaction	交易
hawk	主戰派份子
dove	主和派份子，和平鴿
president	總統
PM; Prime Minister	總理，首相
vice president	副總統
acting president	代總統
administration party	執政黨
party in power	執政黨
party in opposition	在野黨
conservative party	保守黨
assembly hall	會議廳
senate	參議院
parliament	國會
body, committee, commission	
	組織，委員會
c'tee	委員會(簡寫)
One-country-two-system policy	
	一國兩制的政策
protocol	草案，協議

map	制訂
work out	制訂
anarchy	無政府狀態
overwhelming majority	壓倒性多數
negative vote	反對票
positive vote	贊成票
roll-call vote	點名投票
voting card	投票卡
voting observer	監票員
speaker	議長
deputy speaker	副議長
congressman	男國會議員
congresswoman	女國會議員
senator	參議員
mayor	市長
incumbent mayor	現任市長
county magistrate	縣長
township head	鄉長
village master	村長
town master	鎮長
rep; representative	代表
politician	政客
tenure of office	任職期
township enterprises	鄉鎮企業
press spokesman	新聞發言人
spokesman	發言人
civilian	平民

cabinet reshuffle	內閣改組
cabinet lineup	內閣陣容
brain trust	智囊團
official	官員
bureaucrat	官僚
bureaucracy	官僚主義
bribery	行賄
amnesty	特赦
blanket ballot	全面選舉
poll, election	投票選舉，民意測驗
nominee	候選人
constituency	選區，選民
ballot	選票，投票
arch-foe	主要的勁敵
vow	決心，發誓
step down	辭職，下臺
depose	罷免
anti-corruption	反腐敗
presidential election	總統選舉
inaugural address	就職演說
bullet	子彈
name, appoint	命名，提名
nominate	命名，提名
election	選舉
text message	文字簡訊
assassinate	暗殺行刺

plebiscite, referendum	公投
purchase arms	購買武器
anti-secession law	反分裂法
independence	獨立
reunification	統一
Aussie; Australian	澳大利亞的
Russ; Russia	俄羅斯，現為獨立國協一員

外交新聞

foreign ministry spokesman	外交部發言人
ambassador	大使
ambassadress	大使夫人
envoy	大使
ties, relations	外交關係
bluff diplomacy	恫嚇外交
diplomacy	外交

商業財經

biz	商業
business	商業
knowledge economy	知識經濟
economic take-off	經濟起飛
economic sanction	經濟制裁
climb out	經濟復蘇
bottom out	走出低谷
bubble economy	泡沫經濟
floor trader	場內交易人

operating margin	營運利潤
shortfall	不足，差額，赤字
hedge fund	對沖基金，投機性的投資團體
anti-trust	反托拉斯
balance sheet	資產負債表
borrower	債方
inventory	貨存，庫存量
mutual fund	共同基金
active capital	流動資本
active trade balance	順差
adverse trade balance	逆差
daily turnover	日成交量
closing price	收盤價
stake	股份，利害關係
black market price	黑市價
boycott	聯合抵制
boost	增加，提高
boom	(經濟)繁榮，興旺
soar	急劇上升
ceiling price	最高限價
lop	下降，減少
dip	下降
axe	解雇，減少
plunge	價格等暴跌
plummet	價格等暴跌
trim	削減

ease	減輕，緩和
end	結束，中止
terminate	結束，中止
freeze	凍結，平穩
bottle up	抑制
glut	供過於求
supply-demand imbalance	供求失調
bid up price	哄抬物價
financial quarters	金融界方面
long-term, low-interest loan	長期低息貸款
interest-free loan	無息貸款
inflation-proof deposit	保值儲蓄
trustee	董事
tycoon	巨富
highly-sophisticated technology	尖端技術
redundant	失業人員
re-employment	二次就業
laid-off	失業，下崗
in-service training	在職訓練
CV; curriculum vitae	履歷表
brain drain	人才流失
brain gain	人才引進
labor-management conflict	勞資衝突
richly-paid job	薪水豐厚的工作
hand-to-mouth pay	溫飽工資
on-the-job training	在職培訓，岡位培訓
overstaff	人員過多

娛樂體育

show biz	娛樂產業，演藝圈
show business	娛樂產業，演藝圈
the theatrical circles	戲劇界
affair	桃色新聞，緋聞
box	花邊新聞
sex scandal	桃色新聞
bistro	夜總會，小酒館，小飯館
the other man (woman)	第三者
his-and-hers watches	情侶表
sidebar	相關花架
highlights and sidelights	要聞與花架
pix; pictures	電影
premiere	首映，初次公演
box office returns	票房收入
curtain call	謝幕
closing address	閉幕致辭
box office smash	賣座率高的演出
telly, television	電視機
audience rating	收視率
com'l; commercial	商業的，廣告
DJ; disc jockey	電台節目主持人
album	專輯
chart	(流行音樂)排行榜
hit parade	流行歌曲排行榜
audiophile	愛玩音響的人

cover girl	封面女郎
crusade	宣傳攻勢，聖戰
celebrity	名人，名流
leading actor	男主角
leading actress	女主角
supporting actress	女配角
supporting actor	男配角
lead singer	樂團主唱
invitation meet	邀請賽
knock-out system	淘汰制
eliminate	淘汰
karate	空手道
judo	柔道
guest team	客隊
home team	主隊
ace, champion	得勝者，冠軍
champ	冠軍
sport	運動
archery	射箭術
archer	射手
taekwondo	跆拳道
100-metre dash	百米賽跑
medal	獎牌
umpire	裁判
rapport	默契

社會要聞

criminal law	刑法

con; convict	罪犯
counselor	律師
case	案件
lawyer	律師
solicitor	初級律師
defendant	被告
acquit, be acquitted	宣告…無罪，無罪釋放
guilty	有罪的
innocent	無罪的
abduct	誘拐，綁架
big lie	大騙局
rip off	偷竊
arson	放火，縱火
professional escort	特種服務
escort girl	伴遊女郎
poverty-stricken area	貧困地區
hit-and-runner	肇事後逃逸者
hit and run	肇事逃逸
pedestrian	行人
passerby	過路人
heroin	海洛因
witness	證人，目擊者
nab, arrest	逮捕
hold	逮捕
slay, murder	謀殺
fake	贗品，騙局

phony	假的,膺品
laud, praise	讚揚
bare, expose	暴露
reveal	揭露
assail, denounce	譴責
denunciation	譴責,指責
black box	測謊器
porn; pornography	情色
accuse	控告
charge	控告
sentence	判刑
death penalty □	死刑
capital punishment□	死刑

醫藥新聞

depression	憂鬱症
cancer	癌症
evacuate	使(人)撤離
SARS;	
嚴重急性呼吸道症候群,非典型肺炎	
severe	嚴重的
acute	急性的
respiratory	呼吸的
syndrome	症候群
fatal	致命的
break out	爆發
virus	病毒
quarantine	隔離

isolate	隔離，孤立
plague	疫病，瘟疫
epidemic	流行病，傳染的
contagion	接觸傳染
aerial infection	空氣傳染
bird flu	禽流感
flu, influenza	流行性感冒
virus	病毒
domestic poultry	家禽
outbreak	爆發
migrating	遷移，(鳥的) 定期移棲
monitoring	監視，追蹤 (鳥的行蹤)
bacteria	細菌
V.D.; venereal disease	性病
vaccine	疫苗
mercy killing	安樂死

民生消費 / 休閒話題

anecdote	趣聞軼事
caricature	漫畫
cartoon	漫畫
continued story	連載故事，連載小說
book review	書評
human interest	人情味
two-day dayoffs	雙休日
long weekend	長週末
cable car	纜車
recital	獨唱會，獨奏會

duet	二重唱
solo	獨奏，獨唱
overture	序曲
music cafe	音樂茶座
chamber concert	室內音樂會
concert	音樂會
benefit concert	義演音樂會
multimedia	多媒體
fairplay trophy	風格獎
exposition	博覽會
expo	博覽會
carnival	年華會
quiz game	智力競賽
cultural undertaking	文化事業
modern	現代
postmodern	後現代
modernism	現代主義
power failure	斷電，停電
black out	停電
electric power	電力
deli	熟食店
delicatessen	熟食店
cafeteria	自助餐廳
daily necessities	日用品
botanical garden	植物園
showcase	展示
sedan	小轎車

氣候報導

Centigrade	攝氏
Celsius	攝氏的
Fahrenheit	華氏
the lows, the highs	最低氣溫,最高氣溫
precipitation	降雨量
fine, fair, sunny	晴朗
mild	溫暖
warm	溫暖
cool	涼爽
hot	炎熱
hot wave	熱浪
cloudy	多雲
clear to overcast	晴轉多雲
cloudy to overcast	陰轉多雲
turning out cloudy	轉陰
overcast, dull, gloomy	陰天
wet	雨天
dew	露水
drizzle	毛毛雨,小雨
shower	陣雨
thunder shower	雷陣雨
pour, downpour	大雨
storm	暴風雨
thunder storm	雷雨
seasonal rain	季節雨
monsoon	季風,雨季

sleet	雨夾雪
thunder	打雷
lightning	閃電
snowy	有雪
light snow	小雪
blizzard	暴風雪
snowstorm	暴風雪
hail, hailstone	冰雹
avalanche	雪崩
ice storm	冰雹
windy	有風
breezy	微風陣陣
gentle wind	和風
gale	大風
heavy, high wind	大風
windy and dusty	風沙
gust	強陣風
foggy	有霧
frosty	霜凍
chilly	微冷
freezing	冰冷
frost	霜凍
misty	薄霧
dry	乾燥的
damp	潮濕的，有濕氣的
humid	潮濕的，濕氣重的
stuffy	不通氣的，窒息的，閟熱的

close	不通風的，悶熱的
monsoon zone	季風帶
oceanic climate	海洋性氣候
continental climate	大陸性氣候
El Nino	聖嬰現象
La Nina	反聖嬰現象
global warming	全球暖化
the greenhouse effect	溫室效應
emit carbon dioxide	排放二氧化碳
rise in global temperature	全球溫度上升
glacial	冰河
ice sheet	大冰原
iceberg	冰山
melt	溶解
dust storm	沙塵暴

天然災害

tsunami	海嘯
typhoon	颱風
hurricane	颶風
tornado	龍捲風
cyclone, twister	龍捲風
flood	洪水
drought	旱災
earthquake	地震
landslide	山崩
rockslide	岩崩
mudslide	土石流

221

volcanic eruption	火山爆發
natural disaster	天然災害
calamity	災難
disaster-hit area	災區
death tolls	死亡人數，死亡率
casualty	遇難者，傷亡人員

分類廣告

obituary	訃告
advertisement	廣告
correction	更正(啟事)
classified ads	分類廣告
ads (advertisement)	廣告

其他

on-the-spot broadcasting	現場直播
televise	實況轉播
on-the-spot interview	現場採訪
news flash	短訊，快訊
follow-up	連續報導
in-depth reporting	深度報導
interpretative reporting	解釋性報導
investigative reporting	調查性報導
quarters, circles	…界
educational circles	教育界
judicial circles	司法界
opt	選擇
moot	討論

step	進程，進步
vie	競爭
bilk	欺騙
alter	改變
bid	努力
swap	交流，交換
poise	作好準備
spur	激勵，鞭策
woo	爭取，追求
snag	意外障礙，意外困難
sway	影響，動搖
amnesty	特赦
bolt, desert, abandon	放棄
flop, failure	失敗
no news is good news	沒有消息就是好消息
good news comes on crutches	
	好事不出門
words travel fast	壞事傳千里
bad news travels quickly	壞事傳千里
expert	專家
pro; professional	專業的，職業的
ask	詢問
contribution	(讀者投稿)稿件，投稿
feedback	資訊反饋
UFO; Unidentified Flying Object	
	飛碟，不明飛行物
correspondence column	讀者來信專欄

223

deliver	投遞
PC; Personal Computer	個人電腦
GMT; Greenwich Mean Time	格林威治標準時間
nod, approval	許可，批准
set, ready	準備
begin, commence	開始
aid, assistance	幫助
pledge	發誓
peril, endanger	危害，危及
C'wealth; Commonwealth	英聯邦
tech; technology	技術
vet; veteran	老兵，老手
vic; victory	勝利
Sec; secretary	秘書
red-letter day	大喜之日
Muslim	穆斯林，回教的，伊斯蘭教的
Pope	教宗，羅馬教皇
traffic tie-up	交通癱瘓
mark	慶祝
fete, celebration	慶祝活動

報導新聞常用動詞 - 承認

acknowledge	承認
concede	承認
confess	供認，承認
admit	承認
affirm	肯定，確認

報導新聞常用動詞－補充

add	接著說，又說
continue	接著說
go on	繼續說，接著說

報導新聞常用動詞－宣布／聲稱

proclaim	宣告，聲明
allege	宣稱
declare	聲明聲稱
claim	聲稱
announce	宣佈
state	聲明，聲稱
assert	斷言，聲稱

報導新聞常用動詞－反駁／爭辯

contradict	反駁，否定
refute	反駁
deny	否認
object	提出異議，反對
protest	抗議
contend	認為
argue	主張，爭辯

報導新聞常用動詞－評論分析

observe	評述
remark	評論
elaborate	詳細述說
emphasize	詳述，闡明

analyze	分析道
suggest	建議
imply	暗示
urge	敦促，力勸

報導新聞常用動詞 － 透露／談及

reveal	透露
disclose	透露
say	說
note	談及，表明
tell	告訴，告知
reply	回答

報導新聞常用動詞 － 闡明主張

maintain	主張，認為
insist	堅持說，主張
reaffirm	重申
reiterate	重申
stress	著重說，強調
emphasize	強調

報導新聞常用動詞 － 告誡

| caution | 告誡 |
| warn | 警告，告誡 |

報導新聞常用動詞 － 其他

boast	誇口
exclaim	大聲說，呼喊
conclude	斷定，下結論

explain	解釋
complain	抱怨
pledge	保證

Unit 8　商用單字篇

國際貿易

trade	貿易
foreign trade	外貿
external trade	外貿
internal trade	國內貿易
inland trade	國內貿易
domestic trade	國內貿易
triangle sales	三角貿易
triangular sales	三角貿易
import	進口，輸入
importation	進口，輸入
export, exportation	出口
commerce	商業，貿易，交易
trading	貿易的，交易的
international trade	國際貿易
bonded warehouse	保稅倉庫
free-trade area	自由貿易區
transit trade	轉口貿易
tax rebate	出口退稅
favorable balance of trade	貿易順差
unfavorable balance of trade	貿易逆差
special preferences	優惠關稅
tariff barrier	關稅壁壘

貿易夥伴

manufacturer	製造商，製造廠
middleman	中間商，經紀人，掮客
dealer	經銷商
distributor	經銷商
wholesaler	批發商
retailer	零售商
retail trade	零售業
tradesman	零售商
merchant	商人
competitor	競爭者，對手，敵手
trade partner	貿易伙伴
buyer	買方
seller	賣方
importer	進口商
exporter	出口商
consumer	消費者，用戶
consumption	消費
client	顧客，客戶
customer	顧客，客戶

銷售管道／市場

channel	途徑，管道，手段
commercial channel	商業管道
distribution channel	銷售管道
bulk sale	整批銷售

wholesale	批發
outlet	銷路，商店，商行
monopoly	壟斷
market	市場
home market	國內市場
open market	公開市場
black market	黑市

貿易流程

goods	商品
catalogue	商品目錄
offer	報價
inquiry	詢價
order	訂單
sale	銷售
purchase	採購，進貨
quality	品質
quality control	品質管制，品管
inventory	存貨
stock	庫存，庫存量
foresight	預測
forecast	預測
budget	預算
demand	需求
supply	供應
delivery	交貨
make delivery	交貨
make prompt delivery	馬上交貨

partial delivery	分批交貨
ship	裝運，出貨
shipment	裝載的貨物
partial shipment	分批出貨
commission	佣金
revenue	營業額
turnover, volume of business	營業額，銷售額

開會常用字

presentation	表演，介紹
present	表演，介紹
agenda	議程
procedure	程序，手續，步驟
order	順序，次序
theme	主題
subject	主題
objective	目的，目標
purpose	目的，目標
to do list	待辦事項
task	任務
action item	(會議紀錄)事項
topic for discussion	議題，討論的主題
action plan	行動計畫
outstanding list	未解決的事項
other business	其他事項，臨時動議
summarize	總結
resolution	決議
result	結果

outcome	結果，結局，後果
priority	優先，重點，優先權，先取權
high priority	最優先考慮
top priority	最高優先權
meet (the price/enquiry)	滿足(價格／需求)
meet each other half way	折衷一下
make up (one's) mind	作決定
dispute	爭論，爭執
quarrel	爭吵，不和，吵鬧
argument	爭執，爭吵，辯論
I'm afraid I can't (accept)	我恐怕不能(接受)
be worried at …	對…感到苦惱
it is difficult to…	難以…
it's not possible to…	無法，不可能
condition	條件
on the same terms	以同樣條件
limit	底限
(在外貿業務中有時用來指價格，即價格限度)	
say 5% lower	譬如說減5%
make it $$$$!	算你$$$$ (金額)!
the offer is for 7 days	此報價7天內有效
cost of production	生產成本
be prepared to…	準備做…事
consider…	考量…
long standing relationship	長久貿易關係
decision	決策

confidential	機密
our part	我方
client	客戶
whatever	任何種類，程度的，無論什麼
whatsoever	whatever的強勢語氣
base on	基於
moreover…	再之…
make headway	有進展
appreciate	感激，謝謝
modest	保守
liability	責任，義務，債務
unless…	除非…
subject to	以…為準
final confirmation	最後確認
prior	在先的，在前的
expanding market	擴大銷路，成長中的市場
look forward to…	希望…，期盼…
respond to …	回覆，回應
pass on	傳遞，轉交
strictly	嚴格的
disclose	洩漏
responsibility	責任
furnish	供應，提供，配置，裝備

常見書信溝通短語

PLS; please	請

PLZ; please 請
ASAP; as soon as possible 越快越好
LTNS; long time no see 好久不見
BTW; by the way 順道一提
OBTW; Oh, by the way 對了，順道一提
w/o; without 介係詞，沒有，無
w/; w; with 介係詞，有，和
PPL; people 人們，人
FYI; for your information 供您參考
OT; overtime 加班
POV; point of view 觀點
FTR; for the record 列入紀錄
spec.; specification 規格書
MSG; message 訊息
VIT; vitamin 維他命
DIY; do it yourself 自己動手做
dbl; double 雙份
SOP; Standard Operating Procedures
標準作業程序

外貿常用英文縮寫

DOC: document 文件，單據
C.O.: certificate of origin 一般原產地證
C/D: customs declaration 報關單
P/L: packing list 裝箱單，明細表
INV: invoice 發票
S/C: sales contract 銷售確認書
B/L: bill of lading 提單

T, LTX, TX;telex	電傳
EMS; express mail special	特快郵遞
W; with	具有
w/o; without	沒有
G.S.P.; generalized system of preferences	
	普惠制
DL, DLS; dollar/dollars	美元
RMB; renminbi	人民幣
M/V; merchant vessel	商船
S.S; steamship	船運
WT; weight	重量
G.W.; gross weight	毛重
N.W.; net weight	淨重
PCT; percent	百分比
FAC; facsimile	傳真
IMP; import	進口
EXP; export	出門
MT, M/T; metric ton	公噸
MAX; maximum	最大的，最大限度的
MIN; minimum	最小的，最低限度
M, MED; medium	中等，中級的
INT; international	國際的
STL.; style	式樣，款式，類型
PUR; purchase	購買，購貨
S/M; shipping marks	裝船標記
REF; reference	參考，查價
PR, PRC; price	價格

EA; each	每個，各
CTN, CTNS; carton/cartons	紙箱
PC, PCE, PCS; piece/pieces	只，個，支等
DOZ, DZ;dozen	一打
PKG; package	一包，一捆，一紮，一件等

書信常見詞彙

bear	印有，寫有
parcel	包裹
correspondence	信件，通信
business correspondence	商業書信
personal correspondence	私人信函
company letterhead	印有公司名稱的信箋
address	地址
addressor	寄件人
addressee	收件人
postage	郵資
mailbox	郵筒
overweight	超重
postal code	郵地區號
zip code	郵地區號
postcard	明信片
register	登記，註冊
air mail	航空郵寄
ordinary mail	普通郵件
regular mail	普通郵件

surface mail	普通郵件
express mail	快遞郵件
registered mail	掛號郵件
sticker	粘膠
stamp	郵票
envelope	信封
printed matter	印刷品
delivery	投遞
postman	郵差
seal	封箋
via…	經由…
confidential	機密的
return address	回郵地址
telegram	電報
express telegram	加急電報
urgent telegram	加急電報
telegraph office	電報局
per	根據
per your instructions	根據你的指示
BCC; Blind Carbon Copy	密件抄送
CC; Carbon Copy	抄送

電話溝通短語 – 一般詞彙

disconnect	切斷(電話)
connect	接通(電話)
dial	撥電話
bad connection	訊號不清
poor connection	訊號不清

237

busy, engaged	占線
get through, put through	接通
hang on, hold on	稍等
take a message	傳話
call back	回電
dial the wrong number	撥錯號
have the wrong number	撥錯號
caller	發話方
initiate, originate(the call)	發話(方)
caller ID	來電顯示
identify	確認，表明(身分)
speakerphone	免持聽筒
put…on speakerphone	將…的聲音用免持聽筒放出來
DDD=domestic direct dial	國內直撥
IDD=international direct dial	國際直撥
country code	國家代碼
area code	區號
extension	分機
city call	市話
long-distance call	長途電話
emergence call	緊急電話
free call	免費電話
official call	公事電話
private number	私人電話
switchboard	總機
operator	接線生

information	查號臺
cellular phone	行動電話
intercom	對講裝置
walky-talky	無線電對講機
mobile telephone	行動電話
public telephone	公用電話
telephone booth	電話亭
telephone directory	電話薄
beeper	傳呼機
radio paging service	無線傳呼服務台
telephone exchange	交換臺

股市常見詞彙

public bond	公債
stock, share	股票
debenture	債券
stock exchange	股票交易所
allotment of shares	配股
the main board	主板市場
the second board market	二板市場
stock market	股票市場
list on the stock market	股票上市
stock index	股市指數
IPOs, Initial Public Offerings	首次上市

常見經濟學詞彙

inflation	通貨膨脹
deflation	通貨緊縮

economic cycle	經濟周期
economic boom	經濟繁榮
economic recession	經濟衰退
economic depression	經濟蕭條
economic crisis	經濟危機
economic recovery	經濟復蘇
bubble economy	泡沫經濟
overheating of economy	經濟過熱
macro economy	宏觀經濟
favorable balance	順差
adverse balance	逆差
slump	不景氣
recession	衰退
growth rate in real terms	實際成長率
average growth rate per annum	年平均成長率
rate of return on investment	投資報酬率
total foreign trade value	外貿進出口總額
improve economic performance	提高經濟效益
increase economic returns	提高經濟效益
risk rating	風險評等
attract investment from the private sector	吸引民間投資
supporting policy	配套政策
technology intensive	技術密集
labor intensive	勞動密集
mass production	大規模生產
market capitalization	市場資本總額

| risk management | 風險管理 |
| mutual fund | 共同基金 |

常見國際金融外匯詞彙

devaluation	貨幣貶值
revaluation	貨幣增值
foreign exchange fluctuation	外匯波動
foreign exchange crisis	外匯危機
discount	貼現
discount rate, bank rate	貼現率
money (financial) market	金融市場
international balance of payment	國際收支

常見貸款詞彙

collateralized loan	抵押貸款
residential mortgage loan	房屋抵押貸款
pay by installment	分期付款
installment	分期付款
examining and approving loan	審核及批准貸款
floating capital loan	流動資金貸款
commercial lending	經常性貸款
internal audit	內部審核
internal capital allocation	內部資金調度
monthly payment	按月付款
deferred payment	延期付款
payment by installments	分期付款

跟價格有關的詞彙

price	價格
rate	費率
price list	價目表
price format	價格表
priced	已標價的，定價的
pricing	定價，標價
price per unit	單價
per	每(單位)
price of factory	廠價
estimate	估計，預估
allot	分配（數量）
price tag	價格標籤
pricing method	定價方法
price card	價格目錄
buying price	買價
selling price	賣價
bid	出價，喊價，投標
firm price	實價
firm offer	實價
new price	新價
old price	舊價
non-firm offer	未確認的報價
best price	最好的價格
ceiling price	最高價
maximum price	最高價
minimum price	最低價

average price	平均價格
present price	時價
current price	時價，現價
prevailing price	現價
ruling price	目前的價格
going price	現價
base price	底價
rock-bottom price	最底價
bedrock price	最底價
original price	原價
maintain original price	維持原價
opening price	開價，開盤價
closing price	收盤價
exceptional price	特價
special price	特價
nominal price	名義上的價格(並非市場價值)
moderate price	公平價格
wholesale price	批發價
retail price	零售價
market price	市價
net price	淨價
cost price	成本價
gross price	毛價
estimation	估價
estimate	估價
valuation	估價

discount	折扣
current price	現行價格，時價
net price	淨價
indicative price	參考價格
price is favorable	價格優惠
favorable	優惠的
lowest possible price	可能最低價
highest possible price	可能最高價
wild speculation	漫天要價
price is stiff	價格堅挺的，昂貴的
prohibitive	(費用、價格等)過高的
reasonable profit	合理的利潤
price is easy	價格疲軟
cut price	削價
lower (the price)	降低(價格)
go a little bit lower	降低一點
reduce (the price)	減價

影響價格的原因

term	條件
payment term	付款方式
payment	付款
cash sale	現金交易
currency	貨幣
credit	信用
freight	運費
cost	成本
pricing policy	價格策略

international market price	國際市場價格
world market price	國際市場價格
price index, price indices	物價指數
price effect	價格效應
price contract	價格合約
price calculation	價格計算
price limit	價格限制
price control	價格控制
price theory	價格理論
price regulation	價格調整
price structure	價格構成
price support	價格支援
extra price	附加價
sales condition	銷售條件
exchange rate	匯率
exchange rate fluctuation	匯率浮動
pass over	轉給，轉嫁
bargain	討價還價
trade term (price term)	價格條件
spot price	現貨價格
price including commission	含佣金價格
discount, allowance	折扣

請參考數字篇 – 形容數字高低升降

詢價／報價及還價

enquiry, inquiry	詢價
inquirer	詢價者
specific inquiry	具體詢價

an occasional inquiry	偶而詢價
heavy enquiries	大量詢價
make an enquiry	發出詢價
enquiry about	發出詢價
reply an enquiry	回覆詢價
receive an enquiry	接到詢價
RFQ，request for quotation	要求報價
quote	報價
quotation	報價
offer	報價
make an offer	報價
official offer	正式報價
special offer	特別優惠
offer for	報價，提供
forward an offer	送出報價
send an offer	送出報價
get an offer	拿到報價，獲得報價
obtain an offer	拿到報價，獲得報價
accept an offer	接受報價
give an offer	給報價
entertain an offer	考慮報價
submit an offer	提出報價
preferential offer	

優先的報價，(關稅)優惠的報價
the offer is for 3 days　此報價3天內有效

valid	有效(期限)
expire	滿期，屆期，(期限) 終止
extend the offer	延長報價有效期限
offering period	報價有效期限
renew an offer	延長報價有效期限
reinstate an offer	延長報價有效期限
decline the offer	拒絕此報價
turn down the offer	拒絕此報價
withdraw	取消，撤回，撤銷
counter offer	還價
reply an offer	答覆報價
lump offer	綜合報價 (針對兩種以上商品)
make a bid	競標
get a bid	得到競標
outbid	出最高價

業務行銷詞彙

catalogue	目錄
logo	商標
DM	文宣品
promotional flyer	文宣品
brochure	文宣品
flyer	傳單，單張印刷品
leaflet	傳單，單張印刷品
booklet	小冊子
brochure	小冊子
handbook	手冊

pamphlet	小冊子
manual	手冊
brochure stand	文宣展示架
brochure holder	文宣展示架
sample	樣本
gift	贈品
poster	海報
flag	布條，旗幟
flag pole	旗竿
exchange	交換
business card, card	名片
appointment	約會
shake hands	握手
advertise	為…做廣告，為…宣傳

邀約拜訪

postpone	延期
meet with (+sb)	見 (某人)，與 (某人) 見面
make an appointment	預約，約見
reschedule	改期
notify	通知
cancel	取消
invite	邀請

商品品質

| quality | 品質 |
| quality control | 品質管理 |

quality certificate	品質證明書
qualify	證明...合格
unsatisfactory	不滿意的
satisfactory	令人滿意的,符合要求的,良好的
good quality	好品質
fine quality	優質
best quality	最好的品質
choice quality	精選的品質
selected quality	精選的品質
prime quality	第一流的品質
tip-top quality	第一流的品質
first-class	一等品
first-rate quality	頭等的品質
first-class quality	頭等的品質
high quality	高品質
better quality	較好的品質
superior in quality	較好的品質
above the average quality	一般水平以上的品質
sound quality	完好的品質
fair quality	尚好的品質
average quality	平均品質
common quality	一般品質
standard quality	標準品質
usual quality	通常的品質
popular quality	大眾化的品質

uniform quality	一律的品質
below the average quality	
	一般水平以下的品質
inferior quality	較次的品質
be inferior to	次於…
bad quality	劣質
poor quality	品質較差
low quality	低品質

提出抱怨

claim	索賠
lodge a claim (+with/against)	提出（申訴，抗議等）
file a claim (+with/against)	提出(申訴，抗議等)
make a claim	提出索賠
register a claim	提出索賠
raise a claim	提出索賠
put in a claim	提出索賠
bring up a claim	提出索賠
make a claim with (against) sb.	
	向某方提出索賠
make a claim for (on) sth.	
	就某事提出索賠
compensate	賠償，補償
return	退貨
replace	換貨
defect goods	品質不良的產品

其它商用詞彙

administration	管理
management	管理
organization	組織
potential market	潛在市場，市場潛力
transaction	交易
marketing	銷售學，銷售業務，市場調查
plan	計劃
planning	計劃編制
program	計劃，方案
authorize	授權給…
utmost	竭盡所能
pay visit	拜訪
representative	代表
sales representative	銷售代表，業務員
approach	接觸
promote	宣傳，推銷(商品等)
opportunity	機會
marketing	行銷
survey	調查，問卷調查
adopt	結算，採用(幣值或價格條件)
use	採用…
employ	結算，用…計價，採用…幣值
be equivalent to	相當於

銀行常用字彙

bank	銀行
open an account	立戶
account	帳戶
bank interest	銀行利息
interest rate	利率
withdraw	提款
cash	現金
deposit	存款
remittance	匯款
passbook	存摺
bank teller	銀行出納
teller's window	出納櫃檯
exchange rate	兌換率
payment	支付，付款
pay	付款，支付，償還
dishonor	拒付
cash a check	支票兌現
promissory note	本票
bad check	空頭支票
dishonored check	空頭支票
rubber check	空頭支票
endorse	背書
endorsement	背書
blank endorse	空白背書
cash	兌現
remittance	匯款

| commercial bill | 商業匯票 |
| banker's bill | 銀行匯票 |

Unit 9 　數字篇

應用在任何需以數字形容的場合，如：價格、
股票升降等。

形容數字合理

acceptable	可以接受
feasible	可行的
workable	可行的
realistic	合乎實際
reasonable	合理
practicable	行得通的
attractive	有吸引力
induce	有吸引力
convince	有吸引力
competitive	有競爭力

形容數字不合理

unacceptable	不可接受
infeasible	不可行的
unrealistic	不實際
unreasonable	不合理
impracticable	行不通的
not attractive	無吸引力
not induce	無吸引力
not convince	無吸引力
not competitive	無競爭力

形容數字 - 上升的數字

up	上漲
advance	上漲
turn high	上漲
rise	上升
raise	上漲
rise perpendicularly	直線上升
skyrocket	猛漲
hike	(猛地)拉，舉，提
shoot up	飛漲
rise in a spiral	螺旋形上升， 不斷加劇地增加
look up	看漲
twice of…	的兩倍
lift (the price)	抬高(價格)
(price) pick up	(價格)回升
reach the peak of	到達頂峰…
increase suddenly to...	突然增加到…
have a dramatic increase	突然增加到…
increase sharply	急劇上升
rise slightly to	輕微上升， 慢慢上升
increase steadily	平穩增加
significantly exceed	大幅超越
have a great jump	大幅上升
have a great rise	大幅上升
jump to	上升

go up dramatically	大幅上升
go up	上升
exceed	超越
jump sharply from...	從…激增
improve	改善，增進，進步

形容下降的數字

weaken	疲軟，削弱，減弱，減少
turn low	下跌
fall	下跌
drop	下跌
down	下跌
decline	下跌，拒絕
dip	(價格的)下跌
sag	(物價等)下降，下跌，蕭條
plummet	筆直落下
downslide	下跌
price tobogganed	價格暴跌
decrease	減少
cut down	減價
reverse from a great increase to sudden drop	
	從大量增加突然逆轉急降
fall rapidly between 2005-2006	
	2005-2006年間急遽下降
decrease to	下降到
fall to	下降到
drop to	下降到

drop gradually to	逐漸下降
there is a steady decline to	逐漸下跌
drop slightly	輕微下跌
sharply fall	急劇價跌
fall suddenly	突然下跌
downsizing	縮減
downturn	降低，向下彎曲

形容平穩的數字

hover between…	(數字)徘徊於…
level off	(數字)驅平，把...弄平
easy off	(數字)趨於疲軟
steady	穩固的，平穩的
stable	平穩，穩固
remain stable at...	平穩維持在
remain the same	持平
fluctuate around...	在…之間波動
the vibration of...	的波動
remain at	維持在…

數字運算符號

operator	運算符號
plus, add	加($+$)
minus, subtract	減($-$)
multiply, times	乘($\times$, $\div$)
divide	除($\div$, $/$)
square root	平方根($\sqrt{\ }$)
root extraction	開方

evolution, extraction	開方
square root	二次方根，平方根
cube root	三次方根，立方根($_3\sqrt{\ }$)
the root of four	四次方根($_4\sqrt{\ }$)
the fourth root	四次方根($_4\sqrt{\ }$)
the root of n	N 次方根($_n\sqrt{\ }$)
the nth root	N 次方根($_n\sqrt{\ }$)
power	次方
square	二次方，平方(a_2)
cube	三次方，立方(a_3)
the power of four	四次方(a_4)
the fourth power	四次方(a_4)
the power of n	N 次方(a_n)
the nth power	N 次方(a_n)
is equal to	等於($=$)
is not equal to	不等於($\neq$)
is greater than	大於($>$)
is lesser than	小於($<$)
is equal or greater than	大於等於($\geq$)
is equal or lesser than	小於等於($\leq$)
ratio	比($:$)
proportion	比例($:$, /)
percent	百分比(%)
function	函數($f(x)$)
infinite	無窮大(∞)
infinitesimal	無窮小
Celsius	攝式(℃)

258

Fahrenheit	華式(℉)

數字的運算

addition	加法
augend, summand	被加數
addend	加數
sum	和
subtraction	減法
minuend	被減數
subtrahend	減數
remainder	差
multiplication	乘法
multiplicand, faciend	被乘數
multiplicator	乘數
product	積
division	除法
dividend	被除數
divisor	除數
quotient	商
to the nearest	最接近的
total	總合，總計
round, round off	四捨五入
round down	無條件捨去
round up	無條件進位
carry	進位
significant digit	(四捨五入)有效數字
insignificant digit	(四捨五入)無效數字
null, zero, nought, nil	零

259

decimal system	十進位
binary system	二進位
hexadecimal system	十六進位
percentage	百分點
percentile	百分位數
weight, significance	加權
matrix	矩陣
range	值域
ratio	比例
science notation	科學記號
limit	極限

數字的相關稱謂

digit	數字
number	數
cardinal number	基數,(指 one, two, three…)
ordinal number	序數,(指 first, second, third…)
positive	正數
negative	負數
integer	整數
natural number	自然數
odd number	單數,奇數
even number	雙數,偶數
factor	因數
integer	整數
mean	平均數
median	中位數

mode	眾數
prime	質數
real number	實數
variable	變數
standard deviation	標準差
average	平均數
weighted average	加權平均數
absolute value	絕對值
fraction	分數
numerator	分子
denominator	分母
decimal	小數
decimal point	小數點
decimal place	小數點右邊第一個數字
3 decimal places	小數點以下第三位

商用統合整理報告

by date	逐日的
by week	逐週的
by month	逐月的
by quarter	逐季度
ratio	比例
rate	比例，率，比率，費用，價格
consolidate	彙總
outline	提綱，概要，要點，草案
summary	總結，摘要，一覽
recap, recapitulation	重述要點

stress	著重
highlight	使顯著，使突出，強調
sales figure	業績數字
revenue	收益，營業額
flow chart	流程圖
table	圖表
graph	(曲線)圖，標繪圖，圖表，圖解
pie chart	圓餅圖
diagram	圖表，圖解，(曲)線圖，示圖

幾何圖形的相關詞彙

point	點
line	線
parallel	平行線
intersect	相交
plane	面
2-D，two-dimensional	二維的
area	面積
length	長
width	寬
square	正方形
quadrilateral	四邊形
rectangle	長方形
rhomb, diamond	菱形
parallelogram	平行四邊形
trapezoid	梯形

circle	圓
center	圓心
radius	半徑
diameter	直徑
pi	圓周率
circumference	圓周
semicircle	半圓
sector	扇形
ring	環
ellipse	橢圓
base	底
side	邊
height	高
triangle	三角形
angle	角
degree	角度
arc	弧
cube	立方體
3-D，three-dimensional	三維的
space	空間
volume	體積
undersurface	底面
surface area	表面積
cone	圓錐
cylinder	圓柱
sphere	球
hemisphere	半球

Unit10 辦公室篇

工作夥伴 / 人事行政

fellow	夥伴，同事
coworker	共同工作的人，同事
employee	雇員，員工
employer	雇主
staff	員工
ID card	識別證
lunch hour	中午休息時間
office hours	辦公時間
turnover	人員更替率，營業額，交易額，證券成交額
lay off	解僱
promotion	升職
performance evaluation	考績
evaluation sheet	考績評鑑卡
incentive wage	激勵獎金
incentive tour	獎勵旅遊
incentive system	激勵制度
raise	加薪
salary	薪水

上下班 / 輪班

closed	本日公休
clock in/out	打卡

punch in/out	打卡
at work	在上班
on duty	在勤
off duty	下班
work double shifts	輪值兩班
work two jobs	兼兩份工作
day shift	日班
regular shift	日班
night shift	晚班(小夜班)
graveyard shift	夜班(大夜班)

休假別

on leave	請假
absence	請假
day-off	請假
annual leave	年假
business leave	公假
military leave	兵役假
sick leave	病假
personal leave	事假
compassionate leave	事假
wedding leave	婚假
maternity leave	產假
menstruation leave	生理假
compensation off, compensatory leave	
	補休
deferred leave	補休

職務代理

acting	代理的
acting manager	代理經理
deputy	代理人
p.p.; per pro	代簽
job replacement	接替工作(的人)
job successor	繼承工作(的人)
job substitution	代理工作(的人)，代班者
authorize	授權給，委託
assign	指派，指定
authorization	授權，認可
authority	職權，當權者，當局
in charge of	管理，照料
handle	處理，管理
take care of	照顧

文具 - 筆類

pencil	鉛筆
chalk	粉筆
a piece of chalk	一支粉筆
mechanical pen	自動筆
mechanical pencil	自動筆
pen	(鋼)筆
fountain pen	鋼筆
ball point pen	原子筆
ball pen	原子筆
highlighter	螢光筆

marker	麥克筆，白板筆，奇異筆
quill	鵝毛筆
calligraphy brush	毛筆
color pen	彩色筆
crayon	蠟筆
felt-tipped pen	簽字筆，彩色筆

文具 - 工具類

eraser	板擦，橡皮擦
rubber	板擦，橡皮擦
white out	修正液
correction fluid	修正液
board	墊板
desk pad mat	墊板
mouse pad	滑鼠墊
magnet	磁鐵
ruler	尺
pen holder, pencil holder	筆筒
scissors	剪刀
a pair of scissors	一把剪刀
utility knife	美工刀
thumbtack	圖釘
straight pin	大頭針
pin	大頭針
stapler	釘書機
staple	釘書針
paper clip	迴紋針

clip	夾子，迴紋針
paper clip	迴紋針
compasses	圓規
pencil sharpener	削鉛筆機
sharpener	削鉛筆機
hole puncher	打洞機
calculator	計算機
stop watch	馬錶
timer	計時器

文具 - 紙類

dictionary	字典
phone book	電話簿
greeting card	卡片
notebook	筆記簿
notebook binder	筆記本活頁夾
loose-leaf book	活頁簿
binder	活頁封套
organizer	講義夾
folder	文件夾
paper	紙
calendar	日曆，月曆
post-it paper	浮貼便條紙
scrape paper	便條紙
self-adhesive label	即貼標籤
recycled paper	回收紙
envelope	信封
(paper) box	(紙)箱

cardboard box	(紙)箱
name card	名片，識別證
name card, name tag	名牌
brown paper	牛皮紙
carbon paper	複寫紙
cardboard	厚紙板
wrapping paper	包裝紙
sticker	貼紙
bookmark	書籤

文具 - 黏著工具

duct tape	粗膠帶
duck tape	粗膠帶
thick tape	粗膠帶
wide tape	粗膠帶
thin tape	細膠帶
tape	膠帶
tape dispenser	膠帶台
glue	膠水，白膠
glue stick	口紅膠
rubber cement	強力膠

文具 - 其他

stationery	文具，文具店
pencil box	鉛筆盒
dip	浸一下，蘸濕
ink	墨水
chop ink, seal ink	印泥

| chop stamp, seal stamp | 印章 |

設備 - 會議室

whiteboard	白板
blackboard	黑板
microphone	麥克風
audio-visual materials	視聽器材
overhead projector	投影機
slide projector	幻燈機
slide	投影片,幻燈片
portable overhead projector	攜帶型投影儀
desktop overhead projector	臺式投影儀
projector screen	投影螢幕
photograph	照片
picture	圖片
transparency, slide	投影片
VCR (video cassette record)	錄放影機
video player	放影機
CD player	CD 錄放音機
video tape	錄影帶
transparency pen	投影筆
whiteboard pen, marker	白板筆
laser pen	雷射筆
pointer	指示物,指針,教鞭
laser printer	雷射印表機
electric wire	電線
outlet	插座
plug	插頭

eraser	板擦
eraser dusting machine	板擦機
gavel	議事槌
television set	電視機
computer	電腦
curtain	窗簾
blind	百葉窗簾
rostrum	講台
platform	講台
public gallery	旁聽席
briefing room	簡報室
conference room	會議室
hall	會堂，大廳

設備 - 辦公室設備

typewriter	打字機
fax machine	傳真機
photocopier	影印機
copy room	影印室
photocopy	影印
paper shredder	碎紙機
(public) telephone	(公共)電話
answering machine	電話答錄機
printer	印表機
laser printer	雷射印表機
jet printer	噴墨印表機
scanner	掃描機
toner	碳粉，色帶

scale	磅秤
laminating film	護貝膠膜
battery	電池
PC; personal computer	個人電腦
hard disk	硬碟
mouse	滑鼠
hardware	硬體
software	軟體
disk, disc	磁碟片
earphone, headphone	耳機
eye goggle	護目鏡
monitor	螢幕，監視器
LCD	液晶螢幕
steel cabinet	鐵櫃
fluorescent light	日光燈
electricity switch	電源開關
ceiling fan	吊扇

設備 - 茶水間 / 休息區

drinking fountain	飲水機
water fountain	飲水機
free water served	茶水供應
vending machine	自動販賣機
restaurant	餐廳
gym	健身中心
smoking room	吸煙室
smoking area	吸煙區

no smoking	禁止吸煙
convenience shop	福利社，便利商店
reception room	會客室，接待室，招待室
lounge	休息室，交誼中心
driver's lounge	司機室

設備 - 盥洗室

restroom	洗手間
toilet	廁所，馬桶
close stool	馬桶
stool lid	馬桶蓋
stool seat	馬桶座
toilet paper holder	衛生紙架
toilet paper	衛生紙
toilet roll	衛生紙滾筒
water tank	水箱
soap	肥皂
soap stand	肥皂台
mirror	鏡子
faucet	水龍頭
tap water	自來水
water	水
wash basin	洗手台
sink	洗手台

設備 - 消防安全

fire hydrant	消防栓
fire extinguisher	滅火器

escape sling	緩降機
emergency lamp	緊急照明
evacuation route	疏散方向
exit	太平門
emergency exit	安全門

設備 - 檔案／雜物儲藏室／機房

miscellaneous storage	雜物間
storage	儲藏室，物品儲藏室
warehouse	倉庫
facility room	設備室
tool room	工具室
equipment room	器材室
phone operator's room	總機房
closed-circuit monitor system	閉路監視系統
computer facilities	電腦機房
archive	檔案室
archive cabinet	檔案專櫃，文書專櫃

設備 - 其他

first floor	一樓
second floor	二樓
third floor	三樓
fourth floor	四樓
fifth floor	五樓
elevator	電梯
stairs	樓梯

parking lot	停車場
reserved parking space	專用停車位
bulletin board	公佈欄
notice board	布告牌
billboard	佈告欄
mail box	信箱
sign	招牌，指標
umbrella stand	雨傘架
umbrella holder	雨傘架
ATM; automatic teller machine	自動提款機
vacuum	吸塵器
dehumidifier	除濕機
air conditioner	冷氣
fan	電扇
garbage can	垃圾桶
recycle trash can	可回收垃圾桶
wastepaper basket	廢紙簍

辦公室各處室

head office	總公司
branch office	分公司
Chairman's Office	董事長室
Group	事業群
Division	事業處
Department (Dept.)	部門
Administrative Department	行政部
Customer Service Department	客戶服務部
Finance Department	財務部

Financial & Administrative Department

管理部

General Affairs Department 總務部

Human Resources Department 人力資源部

(HR)

Public Relations 公關

Marketing Department 行銷部

Planning Department 企劃部

Procurement Department 採購部

IT Department 資訊部

Computer Center 電腦中心

Quality Control Department (QC) 品管部

Research & Development Department

研究開發部

Legal Department 法務部

Sales Department 業務部

Auditorial Room 稽核室

mail room 收發室

Unit11 求職面試篇

行業類別

dealer	經銷商
wholesale	批發
wholesaler	批發商
retailer	零售商
tradesman	零售商
retail trade	零售業
middleman	中間商，經紀人
manufacturer	製造商，製造廠
importer	進口商
exporter	出口商
local industry	地方工業
light industry	輕工業
power industry	電力工業
car industry	汽車工業
clothing industry	服裝業
building industry	建築工業
chemical industry	化學工業
food industry	食品工業
oil industry	石油工業
insurance business	保險業
insurance industry	保險業
communication industry	通訊業
enterprise	企業

工作經歷

experience	經歷，經驗
work experience	工作經歷
work history	工作經歷
professional	職業經歷
occupational history	工作經歷
previous employment	工作經歷
employment history	工作經歷
employment record	工作經歷，受雇紀錄
employment experience	工作經歷
business experience	工作經歷
business background	工作經歷
business history	工作經歷
specific experience	具體經歷
professional experience	工作經歷
present employment	現職狀況
position	職位
type of work	工作性質
employer	雇主
period	期間
period of employment	服務期間
responsibilities	工作說明
govt. / state-owned enterprise	公營企業
locally-owned enterprise	私人企業
joint venture	合資企業
foreign-owned enterprise	國際公司
NGO; non government organization	
	非政府機構

學歷

education history	教育背景
educational background	教育背景
academic history	學歷
level	程度
level of study completed	最高學歷
graduate level education	研究所學歷
undergraduate level education	大學學歷
high school	中學畢業
vocational school	職業學校
secondary education	中學
university	大學
college	大學，學院
others	其它學歷
name of school	畢業學校名稱
address of school	畢業學校地址
name of institution	校名
major	主修
year graduated	年度
period of enrollment	修業年限
name of examination	考試名稱
date (from-to)	學習期間
	(從…至…為止)
required years of study	要求學習年限
diploma or degree	文憑或學位
secondary education status	次高學歷狀況

graduated or will graduate from high school / college 已畢業或即將畢業於 高中 / 大學
home schooled 在家自學
degree received 已取得的學位
degree earned 已取得的學位

能力評鑑

English qualification 英語水平
English language proficiency 英語程度
verbal English 英語口說能力
written English 英語書寫能力
intellectual ability 知能
ability to work with others 協作能力
imagination and creativity 創造性
outstanding 非常好
fluent 很流利
excellent 精通
distinction 表現優異
superior 優越
good 好
fair 還可以
average 一般
weak 很弱
poor 不好
no information 清楚

英語考試

TOEFL; Test of English as a Foreign
Language)
托福考試
IELTS; International English Language Testing
System
雅思測驗
GEPT; General English Proficiency Test
全民英檢

工作職掌

employment	工作
position	職位
job title	職位
responsibility	職責
duty	職責
administer	管理
appointed	被任命的
assist	輔助
export	出口
import	進口

專長／能力／推薦

adept in/at	善於
mastered	精通的
good at	擅長於
initiate	創始，開創
well-trained	訓練有素的

working model	勞動模範
recommended	被推薦的，被介紹的
be proposed as	被提名為，被推薦為
referee	介紹人
be promoted to	被升職為
nominated	被提名的，被任命的
excellent league member	優秀團員
excellent party member	優秀黨員

公司組織結構

organize	組織
establish	(公司)設立，建立
expand	擴張
invest	投資
found	創立
registered	已註冊的
launch	開辦，開始
justified	經證明的，合法化的

自傳 - 常見單字

accomplish	完成，成就
implement	完成，實施
achievement	工作成就，業績
break the record	打破記錄
overcome	克服
participate in	參加
adapted to	適應於
behave	表現

demonstrate	證明，示範
perform	執行，履行
project	專案
plan	計畫
target	目標，指標
representative	代表，代理人
succeed	成功
unify	使統一
enlarge	擴大
execute	實行，實施
vivify	使活躍
work	工作
useful	有用的
use	使用，運用
utilize	利用
valuable	有價值的
top	最高的，最好的
replace	接替，替換
receive	得到，接受，收到
perfect	使改善，完美
motivate	促進，激發
effect	效果，作用

自傳 – 實驗設計發明

design	設計
develop	開發，發揮
devise	設計，發明

survey	調查
research	調查，研究
reinforce	加強，增援
originate	創始，發明
regenerate	刷新，重建
renew	重建，換新
install	安裝
introduce	採用，引進
refine	精練，精製，提煉
generate	產生
inspired	受啟發的，受鼓舞的
enrich	使豐富
evaluation	估價，評價
study	研究
test	試驗，檢驗
rehash	重新處理
rehandle	重新處理
integrate	使結合，使一體化
invent	發明

自傳 - 工程製造採購

maintain	保持，維修
repair	修復，修補
make	製造
promote	生產，製造
manufacture	製造
standard	標準，規格
operate	操作(機器等)

284

supply	供給
demand	需求
monitor	監督
verify	證實，證明
provide	提供，供應
material	材料，原料

自傳 – 敘述業績／數字

negotiate	談判
exploit	功勳，功績
create	創造
double	加倍，翻一倍
redouble	加倍，倍增
level	水準
increase	增加
reduce	減少，降低
decrease	減少
lessen	減少
spread	擴大
profit	利潤
cost	成本，費用
earn	賺取，獲得
analyze	分析
worth	使......有價值
total	總數，總額
reach	達到
revenue	營業額
raise	提高

realize	了解，實現
goal	目標
target	目標
market	市場，行銷
promote	促銷
show	表明，顯示
recover	恢復，彌補
consolidate	合併，匯總
reconsolidate	重新整頓
shorten	減低，縮短
lengthen	延長

自傳 - 管理控制

direct	指導
eliminate	消除
manage	管理，經營
renovate	革新，修理
innovate	改革，革新
reform	改革
reconstruct	重建
rectify	整頓
lead	領導
guide	指導，操縱
streamline	使有效率，使合理化
systematize	使系統化
regularize	使系統化
modernize	使現代化
simplify	簡化，精簡

supervise	監督，管理
recognize	認清，辨識
influence	影響
control	控制
significant	意義重大的，影響重大的
conduct	經營，處理
improve	改進，提高
regulate	控制，管理
expedite	加快，促進
speed up	加速
set record	創紀錄
localize	使地方化
authorized	委任的，核准的
break through	驚人的進展，關鍵問題的解決

自傳 - 輔助協辦

type	打字
sponsor	主辦
strengthen	加強，鞏固
translate	翻譯
recorded	記載的

自傳 - 問題解決

solve	解決
settle	解決
complaint	抱怨
claim	抱怨

| resolve | 解決 |
| sort out | 清理 |

辦公室職稱

Chairman	總裁
Vice Chairman	副總裁
President	董事長
Vice President	副董事長
General Manager (GM)	總經理
Vice President (VP)	副總經理
Chief Executive Officer (CEO)	執行長
Chief Financial Officer (CFO)	財務長
Chief Information Officer (CIO)	資訊長
Chief Knowledge Officer (CKO)	知識長
Chief Operating Officer (COO)	營運長
Chief Technology Officer (CTO)	技術長
Consultant	顧問
Adviser	顧問
Special Assistant	特別助理
Factory Chief	廠長
Factory Sub-Chief	副廠長
Director	協理
Assistant Vice President	協理
Director	處長
Vice Director	副處長
Manager	經理
Assistant Manager	副理
Junior Manager	襄理

Section Manager	課長
Deputy Section Manager	副課長
Supervisor	主任
Team Leader	組長
Administrator	管理師
Accountant	會計
Auditor	稽核
Engineer	工程師
Chief Engineer	首席工程師
Advisory Engineer	顧問工程師
Principle Engineer	策劃工程師
System Engineer	系統工程師
Project Leader Engineer	主任工程師
Account Engineer	專案工程師
Senior Engineer	高級工程師
Engineer	工程師
Deputy Engineer	副工程師
Assistant Engineer	助理工程師
Assistant	助理
Clerk	事務員
Operator	作業員
Representative	代表
Secretary	秘書
Staff	職員
senior specialist	高級專員
Specialist	專員
Senior Technician	高級技術員

Technician	技術員
Assistant Technician	助理技術員
Team Leader	領班
Web Master	網站管理專員
Assistant	助理
maintenance worker, janitor	工友
contract employee	約聘人員
messenger	文件遞送員
volunteer	志工
temporary worker	臨時人員
substitute civilian serviceman	替代役男

Unit12 常識篇

標點符號

punctuation mark	標點符號
comma	逗號(，)
period	句號(。, .)
full stop	句號(。, .)
exclamation mark	驚嘆號(!)
colon	冒號(：)
semicolon	分號(，)
parenthesis	括號( ) [ ] { }
brackets	括號( ) [ ] { }
question mark	問號(?)
slash	斜線(／)
dot	點(.)
dash	破折號(-)
quotation mark	引號(" ")
hyphen	連字號(-)
apostrophe	省略號，所有格符號(')
abbreviation	縮寫，略語

世界大城市的別名

Beantown, Hub of the
Universe, Boston
豆城，宇宙中心，美國波士頓市
Big Apple, Fun City, New York

大蘋果，逍遙城，紐約市
City of Angels, Los Angeles
天使城，洛杉磯
Windy City, Chicago
多風城，芝加哥市
City of Brotherly Love,
Philadelphia
博愛城，費城
City by the Golden Gate,
San Francisco
金門城，三藩市
Motor City, Motown, Detroit
汽車城，底特律市
Crescent City, New Orleans
新月城，新奧爾良市
Dice City, Las Vegas
賭城，拉斯維加斯市
Steel City, Pittsburgh
鋼城，匹茲堡市
Bison City, Buffalo
野牛城，布法羅，水牛城
Peanut City, Suffolk
花生城，英國一郡名，薩福克
Pittsburgh of the South,
Birmingham
英國一城市名伯明翰，南方鋼都

美國州名別稱

Golden State, California
黃金州，加利福尼亞
Sunshine State, Florida
陽光州，佛羅里達
Keystone State, Pennsylvania
賓夕法尼亞，拱石州
Lone Star State, Texas
孤星州，德克薩斯
Buckeye State, Ohio
七葉樹州，俄亥俄
Green Mountain State, Vermont
佛蒙特，翠巒州
Empire State, New York
帝國州，紐約州
Land of Lincoln, Illinois
林肯的故鄉，美國伊利諾州
Mother of Presidents, Virginia
總統之母，美國維吉尼亞州
Evergreen State, Washington
常青州，華盛頓
Sunflower State, Kansas
向日葵州，堪薩斯
Aloha State, Hawaii
阿囉哈州，夏威夷
Constitution State, Connecticut
憲法州，康乃迪克

Centennial State, Silver State,
Colorado
百年州，銀州，科羅拉多
Bluegrass State, Kentucky
牧草州，肯塔基
Free State, Maryland
自由州，馬利蘭
Mountain State, Montana
山嶽州，蒙大拿
Magnolia State, Mississippi
木蘭花州，密西西比
Pine Tree State, Maine
松樹州，緬因
Great Lakes State, Michigan
大湖州，密西根

世界重要機關別名

Big Board
大行情板，紐約證券交易
Wall Street
華爾街，美國金融市場
Madison Avenue
麥迪遜大街，美國廣告業中心
Capitol Hill
國會山，美國國會所在地，美國國會
Foggy Bottom
霧谷，美國國務院，諷刺發言人的發言經常模
糊不清

Pentagon
五角大樓，美國國防部
Film Capital of the World,
Hollywood
世界影都，好萊塢
Broadway
百老匯大街，紐約
Uncle Sam
山姆大叔，縮寫剛好是 U.S.，所以指美國政府
或美國人
Fleet Street
佛里特街，英國新聞界，英國報社街
the City
英國首都倫敦市，泛指英國商業金融界
Scotland Yard
小說福爾摩斯裡的蘇格蘭場，指倫敦警察廳，
倫敦警方
White House
白宮，指美國政府或總統本人
Buckingham Palace
英國白金漢宮，英國皇室
Elysee
法國總統官邸，泛指法國政府或總統本人
No.10 Downing Street
唐寧街10號，英國首相官邸，指英國政府或首
相本人
Quai d'Orsay
凱道賽碼頭，法國外交部所在地名，指法國外
交政策，法國政府

世界重要節日

New Year's Day

元旦 - 1月1日

Adults Day

成人節 - 日本，每年1月第2個星期一

St. Valentine's Day

情人節 - 2月14日

Lantern Festival

元宵節 - 陰曆1月15日

Carnival

狂歡節，嘉年華會 - 巴西，

二月中下旬

Peach Flower Festival, Doll's Festival

桃花節 - 日本女孩節，人偶節，3月3日

International Women's Day

國際婦女節 - 3月8日

St. Patrick's Day

聖派翠克節 - 愛爾蘭3月17日

Maple Sugar Festival

楓糖節 - 加拿大，3 or 4月

Fool's Day

愚人節，4月1日

Easter

復活節，春分月圓後第一個星期日

Songkran Festival Day

宋幹節 - 泰國新年，4月13日

Food Festival
食品節 - 新加坡，4 月 17 日
International Labor Day
國際勞動節 - 5 月 1 日
Boy's Day
男孩節 - 日本，5 月 5 日
Mother's Day
母親節 - 5 月的第二個星期日
Lesser Bairam
開齋節，小拜蘭節 -
4 月或 5 月，回曆十月一日
Bank Holiday
銀行休假日 - 英國，5 月 31 日
International Children's Day
國際兒童節 - 6 月 1 日
Father's Day
父親節 - 6 月的第三個星期日，8 月 8 日
Dragon Boat Festival
端午節 - 陰曆 5 月 5 日
Midsummer Day
仲夏節 - 北歐 6 月
Corban
古爾邦節 - 伊斯蘭節，7 月下旬
Chopsticks Day
筷子節 - 日本，8 月 4 日
Moon Festival
中秋節 - 陰曆 8 月 15 日

Teacher's Day
教師節 – 中國，9 月 10 日
台灣，9 月 28 日
Old People's Day
敬老節 – 日本，9 月 15 日
Oktoberfest
啤酒節 – 德國十月節，10 月 10 日
Double Tenth National Day
台灣，國慶日，10 月 10 日
Pumpkin Day
南瓜節 – 北美 10 月 31 日
Halloween
鬼節 – 萬聖節除夕，
10 月 31 日夜
Hallowmas
萬聖節 – 11 月 1 日
Thanksgiving
感恩節 – 美國，11 月最後一個星期四
Nurse Day
護士節 – 12 月 12 日
Christmas Eve
聖誕除夕 – 12 月 24 日
Christmas Day
耶誕節 – 12 月 25 日
Boxing Day
節禮日，聖誕節的第二天，
指拆禮物的日子 – 12 月 26 日

New Year's Eve
新年除夕 - 12月31日
Spring Festival, Chinese New Year
春節 - 陰曆一月一日

重要經濟指標

major economic indicators	重要經濟指標
Exchange Rates	匯率
Lending Rates	利率
Consumer Price Index	消費者物價 變動率
Foreign Exchange Reserves	外匯存底
GDP Growth Rates	經濟成長率
Unemployment Rates	失業率
Per Capita GDP	平均每人 GDP
Industrial Output Growth Rates	工業生產增加率
Gross Domestic Product (GDP)	國內生產毛額 (GDP)
Gross National Product (GNP)	國民生產毛額
Consumer Price Index (CPI)	消費者物價指數
retail price index (RPI)	零售物價指數

國際股市指數名稱 - 美洲

AMEX Composite
美國 AMEX 指數

AMEX Oil & Gas IndexAMEX
石油暨天然氣指數
Dow Jones Industrials
美國紐約道瓊工業指數
Dow Jones Utilities
美國道瓊公用事業指數
NASDAQ (National Association of Securities
Dealers Automated Quotation)
納斯達克（高技術企業板）
Canada TSE 300 Composite
加拿大多倫多 300 種綜合指數
Mexico Share Index
墨西哥 IPC 股票指數

國際股市指數名稱 - 歐洲

Argentina Merval
阿根廷股票指數
Copenhagen Stock Exchange
丹麥哥本哈根證交所指數
DAX (30 stocks)
德國法蘭克福 DAX 指數
DJ Euro STOXX 50
道瓊歐盟 50 指數
FTSE 100
英國倫敦金融時報百種指數
France CAC 40
法國巴黎證商公會 40 種指數
Belgium Bel20 Index
比利時布魯塞爾 BEL20 指數

ATX (Austria)
奧地利 ATX 指數
Brazil BOVESPA (Sao Paolo)
巴西聖保羅 BOVESPA 指數
Amsterdam Exchanges (AEX)
荷蘭阿姆斯特丹 AEX 指數
Madrid Stock Exchange
西班牙馬德里證交所指數
Italian MIBTEL
義大利米蘭 MIBTEL 指數

國際股市指數名稱 － 澳洲

Australia All Ordinaries
澳洲雪梨普通股指數

國際股市指數名稱 － 亞洲

Bombay BSE SENSEX
印度孟買30種指數
Hong Kong Hang Seng
香港恆生指數
Jakarta SE Index
印尼雅加達證交所指數
Korea SE Composite
韓國漢城綜合指數
Malaysia KLSE Composite
馬來西亞吉隆坡證交所指數
Manila Composite
菲律賓馬尼拉綜合指數

單位及度量衡

bag	袋，包
bale	包，件，捆
sachet	小袋
sack	包，袋
packet	小包，捆
bulk	堆，散裝量
bunch	串，束
bundle	捆
belt	帶，條
carton	(紙)箱
cartridge	匣
chest	箱，匣
case	箱，盒
cask	桶
casket	(放貴重物品的)小箱，首飾盒
box	箱
van pack	包裝箱數量單位
wooden case	木箱
van	件 (大木箱)
barrel (petroleum)	桶，一桶的份量 (石油)
bucket	桶
drum	桶
vat	大桶
keg	小桶(容量通常在十加侖以下)

pail	桶
tank	桶
can	罐
coil	捲
cone	筒
container	罐，箱，容器，貨櫃
crate	板條箱
container bulk cargo	散裝貨櫃
skid	(支承或移動重物用的) 墊木，滑動墊木，件
pallet	墊板，金屬或木材之低臺
liquid bulk	(液體貨物)散裝櫃
dozen	一打
lift	一次搬起或運起之量
string	一串，一連，一列，一隊
suit	一套，一副
lot	一堆，一批
stack	一堆，一疊
dose	一劑
basket	籃
bottle	瓶
vial	小玻璃瓶
copy	冊，本
reel	捲，軸
ring	環，圈
roll	捲

segment	節,片
set	組,套
sheet	張,片
block	塊
capsule	膠囊,粒,顆(藥用)
rod	支,竿,棒,桿
stick	支
tube	支,管,筒
strip	片,條
volume	冊,卷
envelop	包,袋
pack	包,綑,副,組
parcel	包,裹
package	件,包
each	每個
cylinder	汽缸,圓筒
panel	板
plate	板,片
slab	板,片
syringe	注射器
rack	架(網架、槍架、刀、帽子架等)
piece	個,片,塊,段,枝
kit	套,組
dozen set	套 / 打
pair set	套 / 雙

frame	框，架子，套
spool	捲，軸
pot	瓶，壺
unit	單位，部，輛(車輛)
vessel	壺，瓶，桶，艘(船舶)
log	圓木
poly bag	塑膠袋
disc, disk	盤
tray	盤，碟
bobbin	線軸
tablet	錠，片
ingot	錠，條，塊
number of pairs	雙(數量)
dozen pairs	雙 / 打
tin	罐
jar	罐，瓶
gross	籮，十二打
quire	刀(紙張數量單位)
ream	令(紙張數量單位)
curie	居禮(放射能的單位)
cut	亞麻等之長度單位(三百碼)
quarter	夸特
quart	夸爾(液量單位)
picul	擔(100 斤)
catty	斤(在中國相當於 500 克，在其他一些東南亞國家等於 600 克左右)

metric carat	克拉(寶石單位)
gallon	加侖
pint	品脫
ounce	英兩，盎斯
pound	磅
yard	碼
foot	呎
inch	吋
kilometer	一公里
hectometer	公引
decameter, decameter	公丈
meter, metre	公尺
decimeter	公寸
centimeter	公分
millimeter	公釐
kiloton	千公噸
metric ton	公噸
tonne	噸
hectogram	公兩
hectoliter	公石
metric quintal	公擔
kilogram, kilogramme	公斤
centigram	公毫
myrlagram	公衡
gram, gramme	公克
decagram, dekagram	公錢
decigram	公糎(十分之一公克)

milligram, milligramme	公絲
kiloliter	公秉
deciliter, dekaliter	公斗
liter	公升
deciliter	公合
centiliter	公勺
milliliter	公撮
square decimeter	平方公寸
	（日本皮革面積單位）
square centimeter	平方公分
square foot	平方呎
square inch	平方吋
square meter	平方公尺
square yard	平方碼
cubic centimeter	立方公分
cubic decimeter	立方公寸
cubic foot	立方呎
cubic inch	立方吋
cubic meter	立方公尺

世界貨幣簡稱 – 亞洲

TWD，dollar	台幣
JPY，yen	日元
THB，baht	泰國銖
MYR，ringgit	馬來西亞林吉特
RMB，renminbi yuan	人民幣
HKD，Hong Kong dollar	港幣

MOP，pataca	澳門元
PHP，peso	菲律賓比索
SGD，Singapore dollar	新加坡元
IRR，rial	伊朗裏亞爾
KWD，dinar	科威特第納爾

世界貨幣簡稱 - 美洲

CAD，Canadian dollar	加拿大元
USD，American dollar	美元

世界貨幣簡稱 - 歐洲

EUR，euro	歐元
FRF，franc	法國法郎
DEM，mark	德國馬克
ITL，lira	義大利裡拉
NLG，guilder or florin	荷蘭基爾德
BEF，franc	比利時法郎
LUF，franc	盧森堡法郎
IEP，pound	愛爾蘭鎊
ESP，peseta	西班牙比賽塔
GRD，drachma	希臘德拉克馬
FIM，markka	芬蘭馬克
ATS，schilling	奧地利先令
DKK，krone	丹麥克朗
SEK，krone	瑞典克朗
NOK，krone	挪威克朗
CHF，franc	瑞士法郎
GBP，pound	英鎊

DZD，dinar　　　　　　　阿爾及利亞第納爾

世界貨幣簡稱 – 澳洲

UD，Australian dollar　　　澳大利亞元
NZD，New Zealand dollar　　紐西蘭元

國家及首都 (A-Z)

Afghanistan (阿富汗)，
Kabul (喀布爾)
Albania (阿爾巴尼亞)，
Tirana (地拉那)
Algeria (阿爾及利亞)，
Algiers (阿爾及爾)
United States of America
(美國)
Washington, DC (華盛頓)
Angola (安哥拉)，
Luanda (魯安達)
Argentina (阿根廷)，
Buenos Aires (布宜諾斯艾利斯)
Armenia (亞美尼亞)，
Yerevan (葉里溫)
Australia (澳大利亞)，
Canberra (坎培拉)
Austria (奧地利)，
Vienna (維也納)
Azerbaijan (亞塞拜然)，
Baku (巴庫)

Bahamas (巴哈馬),
Nassau (拿騷)
Bangladesh (孟加拉),
Dhaka (達卡)
Belarus (白俄羅斯),
Minsk (明斯克)
Belgium (比利時),
Brussels (布魯塞爾)
Belize (貝里斯),
Belmopan (貝爾墨邦)
Bhutan (不丹),
Thimphu (辛布)
Bolivia (玻利維亞),
La Paz (拉巴斯)
Brazil (巴西),
Brasilia (巴西利亞)
Brunei (汶萊),
Bandar Seri Begawan (斯里貝加萬市)
Bulgaria (保加利亞),
Sofia (索菲亞)
Cambodia (柬埔寨),
Phnom Penh (金邊)
Canada (加拿大),
Ottawa (渥太華)
Central African Republic
(中非),
Bangui (班基)

People's Republic of China
(中華人民共和國)，
Beijing (北京)
Colombia (哥倫比亞)，
Bogot□ (波哥大)
Croatia (克羅埃西亞)，
Zagreb (札格拉布)
Cuba (古巴)，
Havana (哈瓦那)
Republic of Cyprus (賽普勒斯)，
Nicosia (尼古西亞)
Czech Republic (捷克)，
Prague (布拉格)
Denmark (丹麥)，
Copenhagen (哥本哈根)
Dominica (多米尼克)，
Roseau (羅梭)
Dominican Republic (多明尼加)，
Santo Domingo (聖多明哥)
Ecuador (厄瓜多)，
Quito (基多)
Egypt (埃及)，
Cairo (開羅)
El Salvador (薩爾瓦多)，
San Salvador (聖薩爾瓦多)
Equatorial Guinea (赤道幾內亞)，
Malabo (馬拉波)

Estonia (愛沙尼亞)，
Tallinn (塔林)
Fiji (斐濟)，
Suva (蘇瓦)
Finland (芬蘭)，
Helsinki (赫爾辛基)
France (法國)，
Paris (巴黎)
Gambia (甘比亞)，
Banjul (班竹市)
Georgia (喬治亞)，
Tbilisi (提比利西)
Germany (德國)，
Berlin (柏林)
Greece (希臘)，
Athens (雅典)
Guatemala (瓜地馬拉)，
Guatemala City (瓜地馬拉市)
Holy See or Vatican
(教廷 or 梵蒂岡)，
Vatican City (梵蒂岡城)
Honduras (宏都拉斯)，
Tegucigalpa (德古斯加巴)
Hungary (匈牙利)，
Budapest (布達佩斯)
Iceland (冰島)，
Reykjavik (雷克雅維克)

India (印度)，
New Delhi (新德里)
Indonesia (印尼)，
Jakarta (雅加達)
Iran (伊朗)，
Tehran (德黑蘭)
Iraq (伊拉克)，
Baghdad (巴格達)
Ireland (愛爾蘭)，
Dublin (都柏林)
Israel (以色列)，
Jerusalem (耶路撒冷)
Italy (義大利)，
Rome (羅馬)
Jamaica (牙買加)，
Kingston (京斯敦)
Japan (日本)，
Tokyo (東京)
Jordan (約旦)，
Amman (安曼)
Kazakhstan (哈薩克)，
Astana (阿斯塔納)
Kenya (肯亞)，
Nairobi (奈洛比)
North Korea (北韓)，
Pyongyang (平壤)
South Korea (韓國)，
Seoul (首爾)

Kuwait (科威特)，
Kuwait City (科威特市)

Laos (寮國)，
Vientiane (永珍)

Latvia (拉脫維亞)，
Riga (里加)

Lebanon (黎巴嫩)，
Beirut (貝魯特)

Liberia (賴比瑞亞)，
Monrovia (蒙羅維亞)

Libya (利比亞)，
Tripoli (的黎波里)

Lithuania (立陶宛)，
Vilnius (維爾紐斯)

Luxembourg (盧森堡)，
Luxembourg City (盧森堡城)

Madagascar (馬達加斯加)，
Antananarivo (安塔那那利佛)

Malaysia (馬來西亞)，
Kuala Lumpur (吉隆坡)

Maldives (馬爾地夫)，
Male (馬列)

Malta (馬爾他)，
Valletta (瓦勒他)

Mauritius (模里西斯)，
Port Louis (路易士港)

Mexico (墨西哥)，
Mexico City (墨西哥城)

Macedonia, F.Y.R.O. (馬其頓),
Skopje (史可普列)
Marshall Islands (馬紹爾群島),
Majuro (馬久羅)
Monaco (摩納哥),
Monaco (摩納哥城)
Mongolia (蒙古),
Ulaanbaatar (烏蘭巴托)
Morocco (摩洛哥),
Rabat (拉巴特)
Mozambique (莫三比克),
Maputo (馬布多)
Myanmar (緬甸),
Rangoon (賓馬拿)
Nepal (尼泊爾),
Katmandu (加德滿都)
Netherlands (荷蘭),
Amsterdam (阿姆斯特丹)
New Zealand (紐西蘭),
Wellington (威靈頓)
Nicaragua (尼加拉瓜),
Managua (馬拿瓜)
Nigeria (奈及利亞),
Abuja (阿布札)
Norway (挪威),
Oslo (奧斯陸)
Oman (阿曼),
Muscat (馬斯喀特)

Pakistan (巴基斯坦)，
Islamabad (伊斯蘭瑪巴德)

Palau (帛琉)，
Koror (科羅爾)

Palestine (巴勒斯坦)，
Jerusalem (耶路撒冷)

Panama (巴拿馬)，
Panama City (巴拿馬城)

Paraguay (巴拉圭)，
Asuncion (亞松森)

Peru (秘魯)，
Lima (利馬)

Philippines (菲律賓)，
Manila (馬尼拉)

Poland (波蘭)，
Warsaw (華沙)

Portugal (葡萄牙)，
Lisbon (里斯本)

Puerto Rico (波多黎各)，
San Juan (聖胡安)

Republic of the Congo (剛果共和國)，
Brazzaville (布拉薩)

Romania (羅馬尼亞)，
Bucharest (布加勒斯特)

Russia (俄羅斯)，
Moscow (莫斯科)

Saudi Arabia (沙烏地阿拉伯)，
Riyadh (利雅德)

Singapore (新加坡)，
Singapore City (新加坡)
Slovakia (斯洛伐克)，
Bratislava (布拉提斯拉瓦)
South Africa (南非)，
Bloemfontein (普利托里亞（行政）)
South Africa (南非)，
Cape Town (開普敦（立法）)
South Africa (南非)，
Pretoria (布隆泉（司法）)
Spain (西班牙)，
Madrid (馬德里)
Sri Lanka (斯里蘭卡)，
Colombo (可倫坡)
Sudan (蘇丹)，
Khartoum (喀土穆)
Sweden (瑞典)，
Stockholm (斯德哥爾摩)
Switzerland (瑞士)，
Bern (伯恩)
Syria (敘利亞)，
Damascus (大馬士革)
Taiwan (臺灣)，
Taipei (台北)
Thailand (泰國)，
Bangkok (曼谷)
Trinidad and Tobago (千里達及托巴哥)，
Port-of-Spain (西班牙港)

Tunisia (突尼西亞),
Tunis (突尼斯)
Turkey (土耳其),
Ankara (安卡拉)
Tuvalu (吐瓦魯),
Funafuti (福納佛提)
Ukraine (烏克蘭),
Kiev (基輔)
United Arab Emirates (阿拉伯聯合大公國),
Abu Dhabi (阿布達比)
United Kingdom (英國),
London (倫敦)
Uruguay (烏拉圭),
Montevideo (蒙特維多)
Uzbekistan (烏茲別克),
Tashkent (塔什干)
Venezuela (委內瑞拉),
Caracas (卡拉卡斯)
Vietnam (越南),
Hanoi (河內)

雅典文化 讀者回函卡

謝謝您購買這本書。
為加強對讀者的服務，請您詳細填寫本卡，寄回雅典文化；並請務必留下您的E-mail帳號，我們會主動將最近"好康"的促銷活動告訴您，保證值回票價。

書　　名：這就是你要的單字書
購買書店：＿＿＿＿＿市／縣＿＿＿＿＿＿＿＿書店
姓　　名：＿＿＿＿＿　生　日：＿＿年＿＿月＿＿日
身分證字號：＿＿＿＿＿＿＿＿＿＿＿＿＿＿＿＿＿
電　　話：(私)＿＿＿＿＿(公)＿＿＿＿＿(手機)＿＿＿＿＿
地　　址：□□□＿＿＿＿＿＿＿＿＿＿＿＿＿＿＿＿
E - mail：＿＿＿＿＿＿＿＿＿＿＿＿＿＿＿＿＿＿＿
年　　齡：□20歲以下　□21歲~30歲　□31歲~40歲
　　　　　□41歲~50歲　□51歲以上
性　　別：□男　　□女　　婚姻：□單身　□已婚
職　　業：□學生　　□大眾傳播　□自由業　□資訊業
　　　　　□金融業　□銷售業　　□服務業　□教職
　　　　　□軍警　　□製造業　　□公職　　□其他
教育程度：□高中以下（含高中）□大專　□研究所以上
職 位 別：□負責人　□高階主管　□中級主管
　　　　　□一般職員　□專業人員
職 務 別：□管理　　□行銷　　□創意　　□人事、行政
　　　　　□財務、法務　　□生產　　□工程　□其他＿＿＿
您從何得知本書消息？
　　□逛書店　　□報紙廣告　　□親友介紹
　　□出版書訊　□廣告信函　　□廣播節目
　　□電視節目　□銷售人員推薦
　　□其他＿＿＿＿＿＿＿＿＿＿＿＿＿＿＿＿＿
您通常以何種方式購書？
　　□逛書店　□劃撥郵購　□電話訂購　□傳真訂購　□信用卡
　　□團體訂購　□網路書店　□其他＿＿＿＿＿＿＿
看完本書後，您喜歡本書的理由？
　　□內容符合期待　□文筆流暢　□具實用性　□插圖生動
　　□版面、字體安排適當　　□內容充實
　　□其他＿＿＿＿＿＿＿＿＿＿＿＿＿＿＿＿
看完本書後，您不喜歡本書的理由？
　　□內容不符合期待　□文筆欠佳　□內容平平
　　□版面、圖片、字體不適合閱讀　□觀念保守
　　□其他＿＿＿＿＿＿＿＿＿＿＿＿＿＿＿＿
您的建議：
＿＿＿＿＿＿＿＿＿＿＿＿＿＿＿＿＿＿＿＿＿＿＿＿

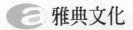